THE ADVENTURES OF
THE FOUR LITTLE MONKEYS

THE ADVENTURES OF
THE FOUR LITTLE MONKEYS

Who Brought Genuine Love and Unity to Maasai Mara Game Reserve

Saustin S. K. Mfune

Editor: Lucinda Hurlow (cindy.hurlow@gmail.com)
Illustrator: Christian Caratelli (christian689@libero.it)

Archway Publishing books may be ordered through booksellers or by contacting:

Archway Publishing
1663 Liberty Drive
Bloomington, IN 47403
www.archwaypublishing.com
1 (888) 242-5904

ISBN: 978-1-4808-5407-9 (sc)
ISBN: 978-1-4808-5406-2 (e)

Library of Congress Control Number: 2017916942

Print information available on the last page.

Archway Publishing rev. date: 01/12/2018

To all those who have suffered the injustices of the world

Acknowledgments

Writing this book was not an easy venture, as I knew that I was dealing with a very sensitive and difficult subject. In my state of doubt, I asked friends whether I should proceed with the book. After hearing the plot and the lessons contained therein, they encouraged me to proceed. The list of those who played a supportive role is too long to mention all of them, but I want them to know that this book is the fruition of their encouraging words.

At one point, I stopped writing for about six months because fear kept getting the better of me. I almost gave up, but my wife, Gertrude, persistently tapped me on my shoulder, encouraging me to keep writing. To her I am greatly indebted.

I would like to thank Lucinda Hurlow for editing this book. This is not the first book she has edited for me. Cindy has the ability to read one's lines and bring out what one really had intended to say. The world needs more Lucinda Hurlows—people who always want others to look better. And many thanks to my illustrator, Christian Caratelli. Without his illustrations, this book would not be this attractive.

Without my personal experiences in dealing with the issues expressed in this book, this volume would not have been possible. These experiences helped me write this book from the depths of my heart, and so I am grateful for them. When on many occasions I was tempted to quit, my faith in God whispered deep into my heart of hearts, asking, "What would my heavenly Father do when confronted with the issues of racism and tribalism?" It is this faith that gave me courage to do what my God expects me to do, which is to deal with such issues with love and yet candidness. This faith did not come about on its own; I would like to thank my late father, Sampson Rhodes Mfune, and my mother, Noliti Nkosi Mfune, for imprinting this faith in my life.

Author's Note

Welcome to the adventures of the monkeys of the Maasai Mara!

Please take note: This book is a combination of facts and fiction. Everything about the Maasai Mara Game Reserve, the Maasai people, and the different types of monkeys is true, but the stories involving the monkeys are fiction. These stories are intended to teach very valuable lessons.

Enjoy!

Chapter 1

Meet Punkey, Lankey, Shulley, and Sankey—the Four Little Monkeys

ONCE UPON A TIME, THERE were four little monkeys—Punkey, Lankey, Shulley, and Sankey—who lived with their parents in the Maasai Mara.

Their home is probably the coolest place on earth—a natural game reserve found 170 miles southwest of Nairobi in Kenya. Tourists from all over the world flock to this place. It takes six hours to drive from Nairobi to the reserve, but for those who fly, it takes only forty-five minutes.

Depending on the time of the year, the Maasai Mara looks as if either a brown or green carpet has been laid over the seemingly endless beauty. It just goes on and on, a magnificent expanse covering 580 square miles. The endless rolling plains take observers' breath away.

The reserve boasts an abundance of wildlife that comes in all shapes, colors, and sizes. It is home to 95 species of mammals and 570 species of birds. The four little monkeys can't help but smile knowing that they don't have to pay any money to be in this place. Unlike the tourists, they do not have to save up lots of money to travel and see the big five: the elephant, lion, rhino, leopard, and buffalo.

These animals can be found at the reserve all year round in abundance. In fact, the Maasai Mara has one of the highest concentrations of lions in the world.

As one might imagine, the air here is always punctuated with a symphony of animal sounds. The four little monkeys can, at any time, hear their fellow apes chattering and gibbering. They can hear the braying of zebras, the bellowing of bulls, the lowing of cattle, and the bleating and blaring of calves. They hear the belling of deer, the barking and yelping of dogs and foxes, the laughing of hyenas, and the squeaking of hares. They hear the howling of wolves and coyotes, the trumpeting of elephants, the croaking of frogs, and the roaring of the king of the jungle—the lion.

In the sky birds make amazing formations. When the tourists see these various patterns, all they can say is "Wow!" Some birds hop on the ground. While some birds are tiny, others are humongous. The little monkeys are privileged to hear the cawing of the crows, the chirping and pinking of chaffinches, the screaming of eagles, the whistling of blackbirds, the quavering of canaries, and the calling of guinea fowls, who sound as if they're saying, "Come back!" Other birds seem to say, "Go away!" As the monkeys listen to all the different sounds, they can't help laughing when they think that some of these creatures would never make it into the choir.

As far as their eyes can see is beauty. The four little monkeys are very lucky.

Although Punkey, Shulley, Lankey, and Sankey all live in the Maasai Mara, they are not all related. Punkey and Shulley are brother and sister, but Sankey and Lankey come from different homes.

The famous Maasai Mara is made up of different areas. These include Ol Derkesi, Kerinkani, Koiyaki, Kimintet, Lemek, Naikara, Ol Chorro Oirowua, Olkinyei, Oloirien, Siana, and Maji Moto, to name just a few. While Punkey, Shulley, and Lankey grew up in Siana, Sankey grew up with his mother in the Koiyaki area. Later he and his mother moved to Siana, so now all four little monkeys live there together.

One might think that all monkeys are the same, but this is not the case. There are many different kinds of monkeys. The Maasai Mara has a wide variety of them, including vervets, red-tailed monkeys, mantled guerezas, and gibbons, to mention just a few. Punkey and Shulley are red-tailed monkeys, and Lankey and Sankey are vervets.

Growing Up

As Punkey, Shulley, and Lankey grew up, it became evident that their parents did not want them to be associated with each other. Whenever they began playing together, it wasn't long before Punkey and Shulley's parents called the two of them and Lankey's parents called him.

One day, after being called away from playing with Lankey, Punkey and Shulley sobbed as they went to their parents.

"But why don't you want us to play with Lankey?" Punkey asked. "He is our friend!"

Their parents said that they would explain why it wasn't a good idea to play with vervets when Punkey and Shulley were older.

Punkey and Shulley, the Red-Tailed Monkeys

Punkey, Shulley, and their parents lived in a hilly place that had lots of huge rocks and a number of trees. There were about sixty red-tailed monkeys who lived in Punkey and Shulley's village.

By nature, Shulley was quiet and methodical and a deep thinker. She had to be probed to say something, but once she opened her mouth, what she said made a lot of sense. She also had an amazing singing voice.

Punkey was noisy and fun loving. He had curly fur, a twinkle in his eye, a dazzling smile, and a bubbly personality. He was a gifted little monkey, incredibly acrobatic and athletic. He could swing from tree to tree like no other monkey of his age. And when on the ground, he was a great sprinter.

Just like his sister, Punkey was also quite musical.

At a tender age, he showed great talent as a singer. He could sing the whole monkey music scale effortlessly. Because of his gifts, he was known by many monkeys from an early age.

Punkey enjoyed eating fruits, insects, leaves, gums, and a variety of roots. His favorite dishes were ants, termites, and bananas. He would do anything to get these delicacies.

Punkey was extremely adventurous and curious and enjoyed exploring. Many times, he had been seen jumping on the backs of wildebeests and rhinos. On several occasions, he had even been seen climbing the long necks of giraffes!

He was exceptionally brave. He could catch all sorts of things, and he liked to scare his sister with what he caught. This annoyed his parents, but Punkey enjoyed it. No one knows how he did it, but one day he caught a boa constrictor by the neck and brought it home to his family.

When they saw the snake dangling in his left hand, they quickly jumped up, wondering what on earth he was doing with such a thing. His parents demanded that he throw the snake away at once and immediately stop his habit of catching things. They told him that it was that kind of snake that had gruesomely killed his uncle some years before. Shulley hid behind their parents, scared to death.

Punkey laughed his lungs out and told his family that he knew exactly how to catch snakes. He explained that it was not as difficult or as dangerous as they thought. His horrified parents watched as he swung the snake around by its tail and then let go. The snake sailed through the air and landed some way away. Everybody breathed a sigh of relief when the thing was gone.

"I wish my friend Lankey was here. He would have loved to see me play with the snake," Punkey said.

"Lankey is more dangerous than the snake that killed your uncle," Dad said.

Punkey's jaw dropped. "What are you talking about?" he asked, incredulous.

A puzzled Shulley came out of her hiding place and asked, "What? Are you talking of the same Lankey we know?"

"Well, he may be small now, but every monkey eventually grows up. Lankey is a vervet, and all vervets are extremely dangerous. They are all lazy too. They like to live on handouts. In fact, vervets are thieves," Dad said with finality in his voice.

"That is why we don't want you to play with him on the playground. He will mess with your good and superior life," Mom said with great concern on her face.

Punkey and Shulley looked at each other, not knowing what to make of this.

"If they are vervets, who are we?" Shulley asked thoughtfully.

"We are red-tailed monkeys," Dad and Mom said almost at the same time.

"Let this sink into your heads: we may all be monkeys, but *we* are red-tailed monkeys, and *they* are vervets," Dad said emphatically.

"I didn't even know that we were red-tailed monkeys and he was a vervet," Shulley said with a faraway look on her face. "I thought we were all monkeys."

"Come to think of it," Punkey said, looking at his sister, "haven't you noticed that our fur is different?" Punkey spoke as if he had discovered a gold mine that would make him rich. "I don't know why I didn't notice it earlier."

"There! You see?" Dad asked.

"We knew you would discover this sooner or later," Mom said. "We didn't want to tell you, because we didn't want it to appear as if we were the ones planting bad ideas into your heads. But you are right. We are different" Mom looked at her children, happy to see that the discussion had achieved its intended result.

"Now that you know, when you are with Lankey, pretend to smile, but know that you are superior," Mom said.

"We got you, Mom," Punkey replied.

After this discussion, Punkey and Shulley slowly but surely began to distance themselves from Lankey.

Lankey, the Vervet Monkey

There were lots of leafy trees in the place that Lankey and his family called home. When they hid in the dark-green leaves, others could hardly tell that there were monkeys around.

Lankey was also a supremely gifted monkey and could sing beautifully. Lankey was large for his age, built like a boxer. His biceps looked like huge coiled springs. Muscles formed ridges on his tummy, making him look like a bodybuilder. Although he was tough and fearless, he did not like dealing with tough situations. When a situation got difficult or challenging, he would easily give up. This worried his parents. Nevertheless, they were proud of him.

Lankey loved to explore nature. He had a restless personality, and this gave him all kinds of little problems.

"You have the body to survive any situation," Dad said one day, punching Lankey's arm with his right hand. Dad's fist bounced off Lankey's bicep as if it had hit thick rubber.

Lankey laughed and rubbed the place Dad had punched.

"The Maasai Mara, though a blessed place that attracts tourists from all over the world, can be unfair. And so one needs to be tough!" Mom said as she looked at Lankey with pride. "It's a place where only the fittest survive."

Lankey winked at his parents and flexed his muscles. His parents smiled as he stood up, picked up a huge rock, and tossed it some feet away as if it was a small stone.

"The red-tailed monkeys despise us. And because of that, we don't care about them either," Dad said, looking Lankey squarely in the face.

A puzzled Lankey looked at his father, then at his mother, and back to his father, before asking, "What are you talking about? Who are the red-tailed monkeys?"

Mom and Dad looked at each other, and Mom said, "Your friends Shulley and Punkey are red-tailed monkeys."

Lankey, disbelief written all over his face, frowned and said, "But, Mom, Punkey and Shulley don't despise me! They love me! When we meet at the playground, we always play together."

"But have you not noticed that as soon as you start playing, their parents call them?" Dad asked.

"It's because they don't want you to play with them. They say that we are inferior," Mom said.

Lankey's face had slowly changed from confusion to anger. "This is a shame! I had no idea that those monkeys think of us that way!" he said as he angrily thumped his chest.

His dad said, "One day I went somewhere to do something. There were a lot of red-tailed monkeys there and very few of us vervets. Then—"

Lankey interrupted and asked, "So we are vervets?"

"Yes," his father said. Both his parents nodded in approval.

Lankey looked at his fur and said slowly, "Okay ..."

"As I was saying, there were very few of us vervets. Then a red tail bumped me as he passed me. I staggered. He looked at me with a belittling expression, and instead of saying sorry, he said, 'That is the power of fur.' And then he proudly and majestically walked away."

A furious Lankey shook his head left and right and said, "I did not know that the red-tailed monkeys were this bad. They are good for nothing. I am happy I have these muscles."

Chapter 2

Growing Up in the Maasai Mara

AS LANKEY GREW, THE TIME came when his parents decided to familiarize him with their beautiful Maasai Mara.

Early one morning, Lankey and his parents walked from their home and climbed a tree near a hotel where tourists were preparing to go on a game drive. "Most of the tourists come from very, very faraway countries," Dad said, pointing at the people below.

"They come by air, flying for hours just to come and see our place," Mom said. "I hear that they land in a place called Nairobi and then drive or fly here." Mom smiled as one of the tourists looked at them through his binoculars.

"Wow! That's something," Lankey exclaimed. "I am sure they spend lots of money!"

"I am sure they do, and they probably save for a long time just to come and see us," Dad said.

Most of the tourists had binoculars hanging around their necks. One group was taking pictures with their cameras while others spoke on their cell phones. The tourists were smiling and laughing, ready to enjoy the day. Lankey and his parents could tell that the tourists were happy to have arrived at the place of their dreams.

Some of the tourists peeled bananas and seemed to really enjoy them. Others cracked open peanuts. Drooling, Lankey said, "Oh! Bananas and peanuts! How I love them!" He stretched out his hand, begging for some.

His parents looked at each other and burst out laughing. Dad wiped tears of laughter from his eyes and then patted Lankey's head.

Lankey smiled. He looked at the tourists and then at his dad and asked, "Are you sure these people have their own country? They seem to be here all the time!"

"Of course they have their own countries, but they admire our place," Dad replied.

"So for them, coming here is a dream of a lifetime?" Lankey looked at the trail of dust a group left as they drove away.

"We take this place for granted, but many people earnestly wish to come here," Mom said emphatically.

"You said something about Nairobi. Where is that?" inquisitive Lankey asked his father.

"I have heard of it, but I don't know where it is. We have everything here, and everybody wants to come here. So why worry about knowing about other places? You see, Son, when you live in the Maasai Mara, that is all that matters," Dad said, a proud smile on his face.

"We have many things to show you, so let's keep moving," Dad said as he swung from one tree to another.

After moving for some time, Lankey and his parents were suddenly confronted with the reality that, although the Maasai Mara might be the coolest place on earth, it was not all peace and tranquility. Some distance down below, hyenas were enjoying the bloody rib cage of some animal.

Lankey and his parents looked at each other in silence and continued onward. Before too long they spotted a python that had coiled its strong body around a fox. The snake was crushing the helpless animal and squeezing the life out of it. Lankey quickly jumped from his branch, which was directly over the python, and moved to the opposite side of the tree. He held tightly to his father's hand, and his dad smiled, assuring him that they were safe. As they jumped from tree to tree, they were just in time to see a lion catch an antelope and tear it apart mercilessly, not paying the least attention as the antelope pleaded for its life.

"This place is kind of scary," Lankey said, fear written all over his face.

"Well, as scary as this place may be, you would rather be in the Maasai Mara than anywhere else," Mom assured him.

They decided to come down from the trees and walk on the ground for a while. They suddenly came to a stop when they saw a big gorilla eating a monkey ahead of them.

Terrified, Lankey gripped his father's hand tightly as they turned and quickly ran away.

"I thought we were related to gorillas!" Lankey said, looking confused as he tried to catch his breath. "How come he's eating one of his own?"

Dad looked at Lankey, took a deep breath, and said, "Son, let me tell you the truth about this beautiful place of ours." He stopped and looked around as if he did not want anybody to hear what he was about to say. "You have to learn how to survive here in the Maasai Mara. Though we are all in the same beautiful land, we don't love each other."

Mom nodded in agreement and said, "We have a history filled with bitter feelings against each other. The hatred we have for each other is deeply rooted." Mom looked at Lankey, hoping that she was getting through to him.

They went to some nearby trees and climbed up again, looking down at everything below them.

"Those with power use it to destroy those who are less powerful," Dad said as they looked at the gorilla eating the monkey some distance below them. "As beautiful as this place is, the most beautiful place on earth, we have never learned how to exist peacefully together."

Pointing at the gorilla eating the monkey, then at the lion devouring an antelope in the distance, and then at the python and hyenas very far away, Dad said, "These animals kill other animals not because those animals have done anything wrong but because this is how the system is. When you are hungry, eat a fellow animal. When an animal strays into your territory and you are strong, kill them."

"This is not fair!" Lankey said, slowly looking up at his parents and then at what was happening around them. No one said anything for some time. All Lankey could hear was nervous heartbeats.

"Son," Mom said, breaking the nervous silence that had subdued them, "I want you to know the law of survival in the Maasai Mara." She stared intently at Lankey.

"What is it?" Lankey asked, rubbing his hands together.

"The fact that we are in the same neighborhood does not mean that we love each other. Always be on the lookout. Just as your dad said, we have never learned to live together in peace. But the biggest danger comes from red-tailed monkeys. You are probably safer with these animals that destroy others than you are with red-tailed monkeys."

"This is so sad! I cannot believe that, even in the land of great opportunities, there are so many dangers and such deep-rooted hatred." Lankey sounded worried.

Mom looked at Lankey and said, "You need to learn to always take care of yourself. If you don't, you will not grow up and become a father."

With his eyes still on the hyenas, the python, the gorilla, and the lion, Lankey promised his parents that he would always take care of himself. "And furthermore, I will be on the lookout for those red-tailed guys," Lankey said.

"That's all well and good," his father said, sounding concerned, "but it takes more than taking care of yourself." Dad stretched his neck while rubbing the hair on his head.

"What do you mean, Dad?"

"Though what I am going to tell you will not be true *all* of the time, most of us know that at the end of the day in this great land of ours, it doesn't always matter how wrong or how right you are," Dad said. He took a deep breath and continued, "Listen to me carefully, Son. I don't want you to misunderstand me. By telling you what I will now tell you, I don't mean that you should go around breaking rules and disobeying everybody. That's not my point."

"Dad, what is it?" an anxious Lankey asked, urging his father to say what he had on his mind.

Looking his son straight in the eye, Lankey's dad said firmly, "At the end of the day, what really matters is whether you are a vervet or a red-tailed monkey. You can count on this."

"But let me tell you something," Mom said.
"What is it?" Lankey asked.

"What is happening in the Maasai Mara is not exactly what our great-grandfathers envisioned," Mother replied, her eyes shifting from Lankey to Dad and back to Lankey.

"What are you saying?" Lankey asked, looking unsure.

"Many years ago our great-grandfathers came up with rules to govern the Maasai Mara. We call these rules the ten-plus-one principles."

Mom continued, "Though their rules were not perfect, they had good intentions for the Maasai Mara. One of the rules talks of all of us being equal. This rule emphasizes in no uncertain terms that no monkey is inferior." Mom paused a little before she thoughtfully and emphatically said, "If only we had put to practice the rules that our great-grandfathers came up with, we would not hate one another the way we now do."

Chapter 3

Punkey and Shulley Learn about the Maasai

AS LANKEY'S PARENTS SHOWED HIM around the Maasai Mara, Punkey and Shulley's parents were showing the two of them around as well. The four of them had climbed a tree and were observing some tourists who were preparing for the day's adventures at their campsite.

Suddenly the tourists dashed back into their tents. Monkeys appeared from out of nowhere and converged on the food baskets that the tourists had left uncovered in their vehicles. Punkey, Shulley, and their parents quickly dived down to join the feast. The baskets were filled with bananas, peanuts, bread, fruit juice, and other yummy goodies.

Punkey, Shulley, and their parents managed to grab some bananas, bread, and peanuts before a fight broke out among the other monkeys over the rest of the food. With their loot in hand, Punkey, Shulley, and their parents quickly ran away. They ran for some time before finding a suitable tree to climb. Panting heavily, they looked back. The tourists were chasing away the remaining monkeys.

"I was getting hungry," Mom said. She munched on her banana and licked her lips. "It is some time ago that we left home."

"I was also beginning to feel hungry," Punkey said, casting wary glances around as he shelled his peanuts. "I am so thankful that our home is the Maasai Mara!" Punkey exclaimed while punching the air.

"Do you know how they came up with the name Maasai Mara?" Mom asked her children.

"No, but I wish I did," Punkey replied while swinging his tail aimlessly.

Mom cleared her throat and said, "It is named after two things: the Maasai, a tribe with unique dress and customs who live in the area, and the Mara River, which flows through our land."

"The Mara River is home to plenty of hippos, crocodiles, fish, and other water creatures," Dad said.

"Mara River! Wow! How I love rivers!" Shulley exclaimed.

"*Please* take us to the river one of these days," Punkey begged.

"Of course we will. It's not very far from here," Dad said, pointing in the direction of the river. "Our home shares its border with the Serengeti National Park of Tanzania. Actually, the Maasai Mara and the Serengeti are basically one great expansion—one great ecosystem," Dad explained.

"I think this ecosystem should be called the Marangeti or the Seresai," Shulley suggested.

"Who knows? In the future it just might be called that," Mom said, encouraging Shulley's thinking.

"Dad, you say that our land is named after the Maasai people. Who are they really?" Punkey asked.

"What do you mean?" Dad laughed. "They are people!"

"Well, I know they are people, but ..."

Smiling, Dad said, "Look over there." He tapped Punkey's shoulder and pointed at a group of shapes in the distance.

Shulley tried to look as well. "Where? I can't see anything!" she said as she scanned the horizon.

"Oh!" Punkey exclaimed. "I think I see what you're pointing at. I can see people wearing colorful clothes and a cow inside some kind of enclosure and some things that look like a lot of kneeling elephants!" Punkey looked at his parents, expecting some answers.

"Where are you seeing those things, Punkey?" Shulley asked, still searching the horizon.

"Oh, I forgot about your poor eyesight," Punkey teased. "Follow my finger and look slightly toward my right," Punkey directed his sister.

"Tease me as much as you want. You know I'm good at whatever I do." They all laughed. Then Shulley said, "Oh, I see them!" Her face broke into a smile.

"That's a Maasai village, and those are the Maasai people," Dad said, his face radiating satisfaction that Shulley and Punkey had seen the place.

"The Maasai are very fascinating people," Mom said, rubbing her tummy. "I like the cloth they wrap around themselves. It's very colorful. They pierce and stretch their earlobes, and when I say stretch, I mean really streeetch!" Mom said, her face contorting as if in pain.

"Ouch! Why do they do that? Isn't it painful?" Punkey pulled a face.

"I am sure it must be painful, but that's what it means to be a Maasai," Dad said.

"And they like to look decorated," Mom said with a smile.

"Decorated? What do you mean, Mom?" Shulley looked expectantly at her mother.

"Well, they wear circular, multicolored necklaces and lots of round bangles around their hands and at times around their ankles. Sometimes they pierce their noses," Mom explained.

"That's interesting," Shulley said as she squinted her eyes, trying to focus on the Maasai village.

"Men usually carry long sticks to fend off any kind of danger," Dad said as he looked around.

"What do they eat?" Punkey asked.

"Their main diet is meat, milk, and blood, but in recent years they have been seen eating rice, maize meal, potatoes, and other such food due to the declining number of their cattle," Dad said.

"And the Maasai don't bury their people. When someone dies, they carry the body into the game reserve and let it be devoured by scavenger birds and animals," Mom said.

"Oh no! That's awful!" Shulley looked afraid.

"Do they really do that? That's scary!" Punkey squirmed.

"Well, the dead are dead and know nothing," Dad laughed. "They do this because they believe that burials harm the land," he explained.

"But there are some Maasai people that are buried when they die," Mom chipped in.

"And who are those?" Punkey asked, curious.

"The chiefs. You have to be a chief to be accorded a burial honor," Mom explained.

"And the Maasai don't seem to fear lions," Dad said.

"I wish I was a Maasai," Punkey said longingly, pointing at the Maasai village.

Dad, Mom, and Shulley laughed, their bodies bobbing every which way.

"Stop laughing at me!" an embarrassed Punkey said, looking at them shyly. "What are those grayish things in the Maasai village, the things that look like kneeling elephants?" he asked quickly, trying to divert their attention to something else.

"I wish I was a Maasai!" Dad echoed, trying hard to control his laughter. Finally he replied, "Those grayish things are their huts. They are called *inkajijik*."

"Inkajijik? What a name! How are they built?" Punkey continued to bombard his parents with questions.

"They are made of mud, sticks, grass, cow dung, and cow urine," Dad answered.

"Yuck!" Punkey said, making a face as if he were eating some bitter root. "Living in a house made out of urine? I can't imagine that!" He looked disgusted.

"Do you see that fence around the huts?" Dad asked, tapping Punkey's and Shulley's shoulders and pointing at the village.

"Yep." Shulley nodded.

"That fence is called an *enkang*. It forms an enclosure protecting ten to twenty huts and is made of thorns from the acacia tree. This prevents the lions from coming in and attacking the cattle," Mom explained.

"It's the women's job to build the huts," Dad said. "And the women are also responsible for providing everything their homes need."

"They must be some women!" Shulley sounded amazed.

"I wonder why they build the huts so low," Punkey said. "Those tall Maasai people surely cannot stand up straight once inside."

His parents laughed.

"I am not sure why they do that," Mom said. "And the huts only have one or two rooms, yet one mark of the Maasai people is to have many children." Mom's face revealed her own confusion.

Punkey and Shulley looked at their parents, their faces full of question marks. "What do the men do?" the kids asked almost in unison.

"They are the ones who construct the enkang," Dad said, "and they also serve as warriors—the village soldiers." He pointed at the Maasai men in the distance. "They provide security for the compound. And boys are responsible for herding the cattle."

"What?" Punkey's eyes popped out. "You mean those herdsmen we are seeing there, challenging a lion, are *boys*?"

"Well," Mom said, "during the rainy season it is usually only boys who are herdsmen, but during the drought season, the warriors work together with the boys."

"Why do the men help during drought season?" Shulley asked, scratching her side.

"Well, during droughts, wildebeests and other animals migrate to the Serengeti in search of greener pastures, and so there are fewer animals here in the Maasai Mara," Dad explained. "Because of that, the Maasai's cattle become a great alternative source of food for lions."

"I see." Attentive Punkey nodded. "So the warriors provide additional protection. That's cool."

"Yep. And you may not believe this, guys," Dad said as he smacked his lips, "but the Maasai people believe that they own all the cattle in the world, and hence when they go cattle raiding, they believe that they are only reclaiming what belongs to them."

Mom nodded in agreement. "And they have a great tradition that I think we should emulate," she said as she pointed at an old man seated in a chair with a number of people around him.

"What is that?" Shulley asked, looking anxious.

"Each enkang has an elder who outlines what each person will do that day, like the man sitting on that stool. He is telling his people what their chores are for the day. These people still respect the elders." Mom wiggled her tail and jumped to another branch.

"I hope Punkey is listening." Shulley frowned at Punkey.

"What are you trying to say?" Punkey shot back.

"You are the one who doesn't respect Dad and Mom. You don't even respect the elders in our village." Shulley emphasized her point by punching her palm with her fist.

"I don't know what you're talking about!" an annoyed Punkey growled at his sister.

"Don't try to scare me. You need to stop your rudeness!" Shulley said, pressing her point.

"Dad and Mom, I think I'm going to go home. I don't want to be parented by three monkeys. Two are more than enough." Punkey sulked as he descended down the tree.

"Punkey," Dad called angrily, "this is exactly what your sister is talking about. She is speaking the truth. You need to respect your elders. Your disrespectful attitude will land you in great trouble one of these days."

Punkey stopped and looked up at his family.

"Time to knock off that attitude," Mom agreed.

"And please don't mess up our fun. We're enjoying the day," Dad said firmly.

"Come back and shake your sister's hand." Mom smiled gently and beckoned him to come back up.

"Okay. But please tell your daughter not to parent me. I know what I'm doing, and I'm big enough to take care of myself without her looking over my shoulder." Punkey glowered as he slowly climbed up the tree. Eventually he looked at Shulley. He smiled as he stretched out his hand and joked, "If you weren't my sister, I wouldn't be doing this."

Shulley giggled as she stretched out her hand as well. Mom hugged both of them.

"We must have missed some activity at the Maasai village," Shulley said as they looked back at the village.

"It looks like they're finished distributing the work," Punkey observed.

"I think you're right," Shulley said.

The Maasai village buzzed with all kinds of activity like a busy beehive. Some tourist vehicles meandered along the road and stopped by the village. The tourists climbed down from their vehicles and began to mingle with the villagers.

"The Maasai are used to this," Dad said. "They see these tourists all the time."

The tourists' hands moved up and down, and the villagers responded in a similar manner.

"What language do they speak?" Punkey looked inquisitively at his parents.

"The tourists or the Maasai?" Shulley teased Punkey.

"Shulley, I'm not asking you!" Punkey frowned at her.

"I'm only kidding! Why are you so worked up?" Shulley looked at her parents for support.

"Punkey, your sister is only seeking some clarification," Dad said, trying to ease the tension.

"Okay, Dad. I meant the Maasai people," Punkey grumbled. "What language do they speak?"

"Maa is their language," Dad answered.

"Do the tourists know the Maa language?" Punkey asked.

"I doubt that," Dad said. "But through hand signs they are able to understand one another."

After a short time, the Maasai gathered in a circle and began to sing. Then the men, one by one, jumped straight up in the air while holding their sticks in their hands.

"What is that?" Shulley and Punkey asked at the same time, both curious.

"That is a dance jump," Dad said, first looking at the children and then at the dancers. "It is called *adumu*. Traditionally, it is a graduation dance."

"Graduation dance?" Punkey's eyes nearly popped out of their sockets.

"Yes," Dad said. "It is performed when boys have successfully gone through the circumcision ceremony and marks their graduation from boyhood to manhood. But as you can see, right now they are only doing it for the tourists so that they can get some money."

"These are very interesting people," Punkey observed.

"Interesting indeed," Mom agreed.

As Shulley and Punkey looked at the village, something caught their attention. Some of the Maasai herdsmen had left the enkang to graze their cattle, and there were a few lions not far from them.

"Look at that!" Punkey shouted as he pointed at the herdsmen. "How can they do that?"

"As your dad told you, the Maasai don't seem to fear lions. Of all the animals, they mostly fear buffalos. They don't mess with them."

"Wow! Grazing cattle next to lions looks very cool. I surely would like to try that," Punkey said, his eyes dancing with excitement.

"Try what?" Shulley exclaimed.

His parents looked at him, laughed nervously, and told him in no uncertain terms that on the day he tried that, scavenging vultures would finish what the lions left of him. They told him that no one understands how the Maasai herdsmen can do it all the time without fear of being killed.

The Maasai people headed off with their cattle, leaving the lions lying lazily in the grass. After a short time, from behind an anthill, a lion roared, and then a cow's low of pain filled the air. In a flash, Maasai men came from every direction carrying their sticks and spears. Like lightning they bolted toward the anthill.

"What can sticks and spears do to a lion?" Punkey mocked.

But it did not take long for him to swallow his words. The lion roared again as it fled for its life. The cow was rescued.

"These people are something else," Punkey said, struggling to believe what he had just witnessed.

Dad said, "When it comes to the Maasai, don't mess with their cattle. Their cattle are of great value to them. Their prayer is *'Meishoo iyiook enkai inkishu o-nkera,'* which means, 'May the Creator give us cattle and children.' This tells us that their cattle means a lot to them."

"Hey, Dad, look over there! Look at those wild dogs!" Punkey exclaimed excitedly.

"Oh no!" Shulley could not believe what she was seeing. The wild dogs were chasing a gazelle and eating it alive as it ran. It did not take much time before the gazelle collapsed.

"And look at that lion over there carrying its kill," Shulley said. She looked frightened.

"Such is life here in our beautiful Maasai Mara," Dad said sadly.

"Unbelievable!" Punkey sighed.

Dad shook his head and said, "I couldn't help thinking of vervets when I saw those wild dogs eating that gazelle."

"What do you mean, Dad?" Shulley asked.

"Vervets are dangerous," Dad said.

"You told us that, but surely they don't eat things alive like those wild dogs do?" a restless Punkey nagged.

"They seem to find joy in killing. Many red tails have been killed by vervets. But what is puzzling is that they kill each other more than they kill us." Dad shrugged his shoulders.

"We cannot say it enough—never trust a vervet!" Mom concluded the discussion.

Chapter 4

Punkey, Shulley, and Lankey Continue to Learn from Their Parents

AS PUNKEY, SHULLEY, AND THEIR parents continued on their sightseeing journey, they saw a group of vervet monkeys on their way somewhere.

Mom quickly beckoned to the two children. "As we have told you before, although those are monkeys like us," she said, pausing to see if Punkey and Shulley were listening, "they are vervet monkeys, and we are red-tailed monkeys."

Dad continued, "For the sake of emphasis, I would like to repeat that they are worse than the wild dogs you saw eating that gazelle." Dad shook his head to emphasize what he had just said.

"I mean it. We are not trying to teach you evil things, but vervets generally have bad characters. No one understands why. We try to avoid them even though we don't say it publicly."

Punkey and Shulley eyed the vervets, who did not seem to notice them.

"Honestly, Dad, do you really mean they are worse than the animals we saw eating other animals?" Punkey continued to eye the vervet monkeys.

"Absolutely!" Dad nodded.

"So … ah … who can be trusted?" a confused Punkey asked.

His parents looked at each other. Then Mom said, "It may sound terrible, but you are safer with wild dogs than vervets."

A surprised Shulley raised her eyebrows. "Are vervets really that bad?"

"Yes." Dad nodded again, supporting what his wife had said.

"Is there a system that can protect us from these dumb and terrible vervets?" a visibly anxious Punkey asked.

"There is a system," Dad quickly answered, looking straight into Punkey's eyes. "There are monkeys who are employed to protect us—the Monkey Protection Force, or the MPF for short. But, Son, vervets are complex. Even the MPF doesn't know how to handle them. There is more to vervets than meets the eye."

"The MPF is composed of both red-tailed monkeys and vervets. Originally we all hoped that this would slow down the bad behavior of the vervets, but it's not working," Mom said, sounding helpless. She took a deep breath and continued, "What is scarier is that these vervets are lowering the value of our beautiful Maasai Mara!"

"In fact, there is an organization among us red tails that has been working hard to wipe out vervets from the Maasai Mara—the Wipe Out the Vervets Organization, popularly known as WOTVO," Dad said. "There are some red-tailed monkeys who don't agree with everything WOTVO says and does against vervets, but, hey, I know where WOTVO is coming from, and I understand."

"I wish they would succeed in killing all the vervets!" Wrinkles of anger creased Punkey's face. "If I was big like you, Dad," Punkey said, pointing at his dad, "I would have joined WOTVO."

"Maybe you will someday. Who knows?" Dad looked at Punkey. "But you don't have to join the group to make a difference. You can still achieve the same purposes but in a more subtle way."

"How do I do that?" Punkey was intrigued.

Dad looked at Lankey thoughtfully, then said, "Be patient. As you grow up, such opportunities will present themselves to you."

"But, Dad, are vervets really wrong *all* the time?" Shulley asked.

"Uh ... well ... maybe not. You've asked a good question, Shulley. Vervets are probably not totally evil. Some of what is going on, I think, is just hatred that has been passed from one generation to the other," Dad replied.

Lankey Learns Details of the Red-Tailed Monkeys

In another corner of the Maasai Mara, Lankey was enjoying the expedition with his parents. As they continued with their journey, Lankey looked at his parents and said, "It has been a great day, Dad!" He looked around in satisfaction. "So far, so good."

"Thank you," Dad said.

"I am happy you have enjoyed the day," Mom added.

"Yep, I have learned a lot!" Lankey nodded.

They heard some barking and turned to look in the direction of the sound. In the distance some red-tailed monkeys were teaching their kids to jump from branch to branch. "Until you told me about those red-tailed guys, I thought that we were the same," Lankey said, looking suspiciously at the troop.

Dad and Mom looked into Lankey's eyes. Dad said, "As a matter of fact, as you grow up, you will learn even more things about those guys. As we have told you over and over, those red tails despise us. They think we are nothing. They think that just because we are vervets, we are inferior!" Dad's chest heaved up and down with frustration as he spoke. "Many of our kind have suffered and some have even been killed because of them." Dad paused a moment and then said, "I know I'm repeating myself, but I want this to sink into your mind. Do you remember the animals we saw eating other animals?"

Lankey nodded as he said, "I am safer with those killers than the proud red-tailed guys."

Mom, holding Lankey's hands, said, "Yes, you are."

"And though we have taught you to be gentle," Dad whispered, as if afraid that somebody would eavesdrop, "that counsel does not include them."

"Don't allow them to use you as a doormat. Be tough!" Mom squeezed Lankey's hands.

Dad looked sternly at Lankey and asked, "What has your mom just said?"

"Be tough," Lankey replied as he flexed his muscles. His parents nodded in approval.

Lankey looked at his parents and asked, "Is there no system that can protect us from these evil red-tailed monsters?"

Dad and Mom looked at each other. Then Mom said, "There is an organization of monkeys called the Monkey Protection Force, or the MPF."

"So why don't they do their job?" Lankey asked.

Dad said passionately, "Son, this issue goes beyond an organization. You see, the organization is just a name, and the issue we are dealing with here goes beyond a name. It is an issue that has its roots in the heart. If hearts are not changed, there is no organization that can succeed."

Mom held Lankey's shoulder, looked around suspiciously, and said, "Many times we've wasted time fighting each other rather than fighting our real enemies. I have heard of cases where it is believed that innocent monkeys were killed by the same monkeys who were supposed to protect them, be it vervets or red tails."

"But that doesn't make sense!" Lankey looked at his father, his face full of questions. "Or does it?"

"Well, it doesn't make sense, but that is reality," Dad replied.

"But why can't the MPF be more careful when doing their job?" Lankey asked.

"I don't know. It is very distressing when someone you feel is innocent is killed. In many cases, the MPF tells us that they have to make serious decisions in a fraction of a second," Mom lamented.

Lankey looked at his mother and slowly asked, "Do you mean to say that the MPF has only killed vervets?"

"That is not what your mother is saying," Dad said. "Red-tailed monkeys have definitely been killed by the MPF as well. No question about it. But in all fairness it seems as if more vervets have suffered injustice at the hands of the MPF than red-tailed monkeys. But I could be wrong," Dad said, shrugging his shoulders.

Chapter 5

Lankey Visits the Mara River

ONE DAY, IN THE MONTH of August, Lankey's parents took him to the Mara River. From a perch in a tree not far from the river, they watched the many activities going on in the Maasai Mara. In the river, several grayish logs were floating by. Lankey's curiosity got the better of him, and he decided to surprise his family. While his parents were watching some tourists on the opposite side of the river, he quietly came down from the tree and jumped onto one of the logs. He began to sing, waving his hands up in the air, having the time of his life.

Instead of being surprised and pleased as he had hoped, Lankey's horrified parents screamed at him to get off. He was not riding a log—he was on the back of a crocodile! Just then, all the other "logs" swam around the "log" that Lankey was floating on and opened their mouths, displaying their long, sharp teeth. Terrified, Lankey screamed, leaped in the air, and landed on the shore, his heart beating wildly. He was lucky to be alive.

He quickly climbed up the tree and joined his parents. He got a good, hard talking-to. His frightened mom reminded him of what she had told him before: if he was not careful, he would not become a father; he would die. Lankey looked down in shame and promised not to do such a foolish thing again. His mother hugged and comforted him.

While still up in the tree, they saw thousands of wildebeests coming toward the Mara River. The herd looked like a huge moving blanket covering the ground.

"What's going on?" Lankey asked, his eyes wide.

"This is the great migration," his mother replied.

"The great what?" Lankey asked, scanning the wide expanse of animals.

"The great migration," his father said.

"What is that?" Lankey asked inquisitively.

His father took a deep breath and said, "Between the months of July and October, wildebeests and some other animals return to the Maasai Mara from the Serengeti. When there are no rains here, they go to the Serengeti in search of food. And while in the Serengeti, between February and March, they give birth to thousands of calves. Then between July and October, they leave the southern plains of the Serengeti and head north to the Maasai Mara."

"Wow!" Lankey said.

"While they're in the Serengeti, the Maasai Mara receives rain between April and early May, and the grass grows again. That is why you see them returning, because they now have food here."

"Does anybody know how many animals are involved in the migration?" Lankey asked.

His father looked at his mom and said, "You're the one who is good with numbers."

"About two million animals make the migration every year," Mom said.

As they spoke, Lankey spotted some zebras and Thomson's gazelles making the great migration as well. Of course, there were not as many of them as there were wildebeests.

"That is a lot of animals!" Lankey exclaimed as the animals neared the river. Then he looked at the river in alarm. "Look at those crocodiles in the river. They're waiting for the animals! Oh no! Somebody should warn the wildebeests."

But it was too late. The migrating animals began splashing into the river.

The crocodiles came alive. They pounced on the animals and thrashed them violently until blood filled the water.

"Though the crocodiles kill lots of these animals as they cross the Mara River," Dad said, "one hardly notices the difference, as there are so many of them."

Chapter 6

Punkey, Shulley, and Lankey Go to School

WHEN PUNKEY AND SHULLEY GREW old enough, they started attending the school, which was about a mile from their home. Before their first day, their parents warned them that there would be vervets at school and that, as such, they should continually be on the alert. Their parents encouraged them to choose friends only among the red tails.

Due to his outgoing personality and musical and sporting abilities, Punkey was an instant hit with his schoolmates. He became like a celebrity, and as a result he enjoyed school a lot. Shulley also enjoyed school but for different reasons. She was a good learner and quickly became known as an A student at the school.

Just as their parents had warned them, there were a good number of vervets at the school. It did not take long for Punkey and Shulley to notice that, although there were other kinds of monkeys at the school, the biggest rivalry was between the vervets and the red-tailed monkeys.

While Shulley was serious about her schoolwork, Punkey, though he had great academic potential, had two little problems. First, he loved playing more than listening to Miss Pam, his class teacher. Second, he hated doing his homework. Because of these two things, he got mostly Cs and the occasional B when he should have been getting As. Punkey would often boast about getting Bs on tests without even studying. He warned his classmates that the day he *did* study they would get the shock of their lives. He told them that he was an academic sleeping giant.

But in general, Punkey was an all-rounder. He was good at all kinds of activities and, as a result, began to acquire lots of trophies.

In addition, his musical abilities meant that the school always chose him to sing the monkey national anthem whenever government officials came to visit the school or whenever there were big school functions.

As one year turned into two, then three, then four years, Punkey's popularity and influence grew even more. Older students aligned themselves with him, and together they became champions of bullying other monkeys, especially vervets.

Lankey at School

The same year that Punkey and Shulley started school, Lankey also started school. Before he and his parents left for school, his parents gave him a pep talk.

"There are two things I would like to share with you as you start school," his father said.

"What is it, Dad?"

"You are a great guy, but many times when things are tough, you quickly give up," Dad said, a serious look on his face.

Mom joined in. "You will need to be persistent at school, Lankey. You need to work hard," she chided.

"Okay, Mom and Dad. I hear you. I will work hard."

"The second thing I need to tell you is that you will meet a lot of red-tailed monkeys at school." Dad looked straight into Lankey's eyes.

Lankey smiled as he showed his parents his biceps and said, "I have heard enough of how those red tails feel about us. I used to think that Punkey and Shulley were my friends, but I didn't know then what they think of us." He bit his lower lip as he bounced his fists together.

As Lankey walked with his parents to the principal's office to be registered, some children pointed at him and giggled, and others made demeaning remarks.

"This is what I meant," Dad whispered to Lankey.

"Don't worry, Dad. I will handle this," Lankey assured his dad. Looking at his parents, he said, "If anyone tries to mess with me, all hell will break loose here!" Lankey's teeth were chattering against each other he was so angry. He grabbed a small shrub and yanked it out of the ground.

"That's my boy!" Dad sounded proud.

After they finished the registration, Lankey's parents returned home, and the principal took Lankey to his class. The principal knocked, opened the door, and beckoned to Lankey's teacher, Miss Pam, to come outside. She whispered something in Miss Pam's ear and walked away. Miss Pam shook Lankey's hand and ushered him into the class. As soon as they walked in, there was a murmur in the room. Miss Pam introduced Lankey to the class.

"Lankey, before you go to your seat, which is over there," Miss Pam said, pointing at an empty seat, "could you please briefly tell the class something about yourself?"

He looked at the class and said, "My name is Lankey. I've noticed your attitude toward me. Well, if this is the way you have been treating other vervets, you are in for a rude awakening. I will not tolerate that kind of nonsense." He paused and took a deep breath. "I will repeat my name in case anyone is deaf and did not get it: I said my name is *Lankey*." He pounded his chest, his biceps bouncing from the motion.

There was loud booing in the class. As Lankey walked to his seat, he felt like a piñata being hit from all sides by rude comments.

Punkey yelled, "Miss Pam, I think Mr. Lankey the Ugly is lost. I have seen him before, and I know who these guys are."

"His name is not ugly," the teacher angrily interjected. "It is Lankey, and—"

Before she could finish her sentence, another student mocked, "His name may be Lankey, but it sounded like Ugly to me. You know how vervets speak."

Another student shouted, "These vervets are suffocating us! There are too many of them. They're using up our oxygen. Why can't they build their own schools?"

A mean-looking monkey said, "Look at them! They might be monkeys, but they are different from us, and I am sorry, but they are *ugly*."

"Should I have an accident and lose a lot of blood, I would rather die than be given blood by one of these guys," another monkey said as she waved her hands in the air.

"And look at him. When I saw him coming in, I didn't even know that he was a monkey!" another monkey ridiculed.

All the red tails cheered and burst into peals of hearty laughter.

Lankey angrily leaped from his chair, grabbed the nearest red-tailed monkey, thrust him on the ground, and stepped on top of him.

The vervet monkeys cheered. Finally there was somebody who could fight for their cause. They shouted and told the class that enough was enough and that they would not continue to take this kind of treatment sitting down.

Tears of anger flowed down Lankey's face as he looked down at the monkey he was standing on. It was Punkey. He left him on the ground and headed back to his seat. "This is just the beginning!" Lankey fumed.

"You will pay for this!" an embarrassed Punkey shouted back.

Miss Pam glared at her class and told them that she did not want to see this kind of behavior ever again. She said that if anyone insulted Lankey or the other vervets, they would be referred to the principal. Then she rebuked Lankey for his violence and told him that nothing is ever solved by fighting. This was just his first day, and she could not believe that he would behave like that. She told him that if he continued to behave the way he just had, he would also be taken to the principal.

Simmering with anger, Lankey settled in his seat. He did not know whether to get angrier, sad, or terrified. He could not believe that he was going through this torture and ridicule just because he was a different kind of monkey.

And as for Punkey, he could not believe that he and Lankey had ever been good friends. He now believed more than ever what his parents had told him about vervet monkeys.

When school was over, before heading home, Lankey met with the other vervets, and they talked for a long time. Some sympathetic red-tailed monkeys came and tried to offer a friendly hand but were angrily chased away.

When Lankey arrived home, he recounted to his parents what he had experienced at school.

"Mom and Dad," a visibly annoyed Lankey said, "no one saw me as anything worth looking at. And it was Punkey, the one I used to play with when we were young, who was leading the other red-tailed monkeys to tease me."

"I knew it would get bad as time went on, but I didn't know that it would be this bad on the very first day," Dad said, gritting his teeth and clenching his fists.

Sobbing, Lankey said, "Dad, you may not believe this, but someone actually said that I was a waste of oxygen."

Dad and Mom looked at each other.

"Why can't I go to another school?" Lankey asked.

"We live in this area, and that is the school you are supposed to go to," Dad said, angry about Lankey's treatment. "We don't have much choice." He paused for a moment and then said, "In life, I have learned that those who flex their muscles survive."

"It is painful for any parent to see their child tortured the way you have been tortured today," Mom said, tears flowing freely down her face.

Dad reached for her and comforted her.

"The day I go to that school to sort things out, it will be a disaster," Mom said as she angrily thumped her chest with her fist.

The following day wasn't any easier, and neither was the day after that nor the day following that. Days turned into months, and the tension between the vervets and the red tails did not lessen.

Chapter 7

Things Get Worse

IT SOON BECAME AN ACCEPTED fact that the bitter feeling between the vervets and the red-tailed monkeys was the way of life at the school and in the Maasai Mara in general. Of course, not every vervet hated every red tail, and not every red tail hated every vervet. But generally speaking, these two groups of monkeys had a deep-rooted hatred and distrust of each other. And as you may have noticed, these two groups of monkeys were not born hating each other; rather, parents planted this hatred in their children.

One day Lankey got a D on a quiz—the lowest mark in the class. When the monkeys were sent out for recess, he was ridiculed left and right. Punkey told him to eat more insects, saying that insects were good for vervets and would help raise Lankey's IQ.

Red tails surrounded Lankey and told him that no one actually feared his hippo-like body. They told him about a series of torments they had planned for him, including putting glue on his chair then he would be forced to sit in it. They warned him that should he tell the teacher about any of these torments, he would dearly pay for it. They said they would reduce his hippo-like body to a pulp.

Lankey, unshaken and unafraid, looked at them intimidatingly and challenged them to make his day. He told them that he had a secret weapon and that they would regret doing what they planned to do. With that, Lankey bounced away.

When he returned home, his father asked him how his day had been.

"It was so-so," Lankey replied, his tone flat.

"What do you mean by so-so?" Mom asked as she moved closer.

"They teased me for getting a D on a quiz."

"Why did you get a D?" Dad's sympathetic expression changed into anger. "You don't study and work hard enough. This is why the red-tailed monkeys laugh at us!"

"Well, I don't know whether getting an A would make it any easier for our son. The red tails just hate us. It has nothing to do with grades. They are not willing to accept that we are on their level," Mom said in defense of Lankey.

"But it will not help Lankey if he is a vervet *and* does not get properly educated," Dad said.

"But, Dad, when I work hard and get an A, they tease me, and when I get a D, as I did this time, they tease me even more. I feel like quitting. I am so discouraged by the system!" Punkey sounded like someone who had given up.

"We have told you over and over that you give up too easily," Dad said.

"Punkey, the one I used to play with, told me to eat more insects because they are 'good for vervets'! Can you believe that, Dad?" Lankey was indignant.

"Punkey is probably right," Dad grumbled.

"School is your future, and if you don't work hard, you will amount to nothing!" Mom looked sternly at Lankey. "We vervets will remain at the bottom of the barrel without education. School is our only hope."

"Your mom is right, Son. The only way you can compete with red tails is to work hard in school." Dad looked seriously into Lankey's eyes.

Lankey mumbled something under his breath.

"What did you say?" Dad demanded.

Lankey remained silent.

"Listen very carefully, Son. Stubbornness will not help you at all." Mom wagged her finger at her son.

"But I need to deal with Punkey," Lankey said defiantly. "He actually mocked my intelligence! I can't take that lying down."

"Since I am busy tomorrow, your mother will go with you to school and talk to the principal," Dad said.

"Thanks, Dad." Lankey smiled.

The next day, Lankey and his mom went to the principal's office. Lankey's mom told the principal that Lankey was being bullied. She did not think it was fair for him to suffer just because he was a vervet. After all, he did not choose to be a vervet, just as others did not choose to be red tails or any other kind of monkey.

The principal said that she definitely did not agree with the way some of the red-tailed monkeys treated Lankey and vervets in general. She assured Lankey's mom that bullies would always be punished. But she also said that Lankey was not helping the cause with his behavior and that it would help matters a lot if he cooled down and let the laws of the school work on his behalf.

Lankey's mother was not convinced. She felt that the school was simply prejudiced against vervets. In fact, the discussion did not end well. Lankey's mom ended up shouting insults at the principal as she walked away, an embarrassed Lankey following behind.

Chapter 8

A New Kid on the Block

AFTER FOUR YEARS OF PUNKEY, Shulley, and Lankey being in school, a new kid joined them. His name was Sankey, and he was a vervet who had moved from Koiyaki. What was interesting about Sankey was that he did not seem to care that he was a vervet monkey as the other vervets at school did. He simply saw himself as a monkey. Miss Pam introduced him to the class and asked him if he would like to say anything before taking his seat.

When Sankey began to speak, it was clear that shyness and bitterness were not in his DNA. Nothing seemed to intimidate him, and he did not have a defensive attitude. He was an eloquent speaker with a melodious voice and a great command of the monkey language. The other students could not help but admire his charming and clever personality. He was well built and confident and wore an attractive smile, and as time went on, the other students would learn that he had great musical abilities too.

Sankey started by saying that he and his mother had moved from Koiyaki because his mother was an entrepreneur and wanted to start a business in the area. He paused briefly to see if he had caught the class's attention. Satisfied, he took a deep breath and said that he was happy to be living in Siana. He had heard of this part of the Maasai Mara for a long time and had always dreamed of visiting or perhaps even living there. He did not know how long he and his mother would be in the area—it all depended on how the business worked out.

Sankey told the class that he was being raised by just his mother, as his father and sister had died the previous year—a year he and his mother would prefer to forget. With deep sadness in his voice, Sankey told his classmates that his father did not have to die. Over the years, his father had cultivated a habit of sniffing the powder of a certain root. Although one got a pleasant sensation from the root powder, it dulled one's senses and slowly killed one's brain. Sankey looked at his classmates and said that he could tell that some of the guys in the class were also using this powder. He said that this was most unfortunate, as the powder had already destroyed the lives of so many monkeys. His dad had taken that root, and a leopard had pounced on him in his state of ignorance, and that had been the end for him.

As for Sankey's sister, the circumstances surrounding her death were extremely painful. Sankey explained that some family friends had arrived from the Serengeti to visit his family. There had been much excitement, and Sankey and his sister had wasted no time in spreading the news to their friends that visitors from the Serengeti had arrived. Pretty soon many monkeys had been milling around—both vervets and some red tails. While the adults were having a good time, the kids had also had their fun. The kids from the Serengeti had told the Maasai Mara kids that though there were many similarities between the Maasai Mara and the Serengeti, they felt that the Maasai Mara was far superior to the Serengeti. They'd mentioned that many animals in the Serengeti dreamed of at least visiting the Maasai Mara one day, if not relocating to the Maasai Mara altogether.

Sankey explained that he and his sister had decided to show their Serengeti friends around, not far from where their parents were. They'd jumped from branch to branch, tree to tree, laughing as they enjoyed the beauty of Koiyaki. At the peak of the kids' excitement, two MPF officers had suddenly arrived and started screaming at them for making noise, saying that the kids were disturbing the peace of the Maasai Mara.

"And for reasons best known to the MPF," Sankey continued sadly, "they targeted my sister. They passed by the red-tailed kids and grabbed her.

"They beat her on the head with a large stick. She gave one loud scream, and that was it. She died instantly. They wedged her body in a V-shaped branch and began to chase us. You could clearly see that they were going after the vervet kids."

An emotional Sankey paused before continuing, "I could be wrong about the MPF officers targeting the vervets, but what do you expect me to think when I clearly saw the two red-tailed MPF officers pass by the red-tailed kids and go for the vervet kids? Why else would they do that?"

Sankey explained that when the adults heard the commotion, they'd jumped from the rocks where they had been enjoying their conversation and came running. When his mother saw his sister in the tree, she'd screamed, "What have you done to my baby?" She'd scrambled up the tree, but just as she had been about to touch her dead child, one of the MPF officers had sternly told her that touching the child would "tamper with the evidence." Sankey's grief-stricken mother had angrily demanded to know why they had killed her baby, but the MPF officers had just looked at her and said nothing. Sankey's mother had withdrawn her hand and descended from the tree. Sankey told the class how, as she descended, his mother had kept saying, "Why is it that vervets are guilty until proven innocent but red tails are innocent until proven guilty?"

Sankey took a deep breath and said, "My sister was never given a chance to prove her innocence."

He went on to explain that his friends from the Serengeti had been totally shocked, as they had not known about this other side to life in the beautiful Maasai Mara.

As tears welled up in Sankey's eyes, he told the class that one full year down the road, nothing had been done about his sister's death. The authorities didn't seem to care. "Because of my sister's death," Sankey said, conviction resonating in his voice, "I am determined to work hard in school so that I can be educated and get a good job. I know if I do that I can help to change some of the unfair laws of the Maasai Mara."

The normally rowdy class was silent, pondering all that Sankey had said.

Chapter 9

Sankey Continues His Speech

IT WAS CLEAR TO THE class that Sankey still had much he wanted to say to them. Miss Pam invited him to go on; the schoolwork could wait this once. She was happy that the class seemed interested in this new way of thinking being presented to them.

Sankey looked at his classmates and at Miss Pam and said it did not matter which part of the Maasai Mara one came from, as they were all lucky simply to be monkeys living in the Maasai Mara. He told them that he once had the opportunity to travel with his mother out of the Maasai Mara ecosystem and that he had not been able to believe the pathetic conditions in which monkeys elsewhere lived. Poverty had carved out a hard life for many of them.

Sankey told the class that as he and his mother traveled from Koiyaki to Siana, all they saw was opportunity around them. No one in the Maasai Mara had an excuse for not doing well, and yet he and his mother met several monkeys of school age just roaming around. When he asked them why they were not in school, they looked at him and laughed. They told him that there were many ways of making money, so why would anyone choose to suffer with school?

Sankey begged his classmates to take advantage of the numerous opportunities in the Maasai Mara. He said that it was the only place where, for those who worked hard, opportunity was there for the taking, yet most of them were so used to what they saw every day that they didn't even recognize these opportunities. "Other monkeys who come from outside the Maasai Mara ecosystem come here and work hard and succeed. Yet many of us who were born here remain as failures, scraping at the bottom of the barrel," he said, shaking his head.

Sankey scanned the class and asked everybody to listen carefully. Every monkey was silent—you could have heard a pin drop. He leaned forward and lowered his voice to a whisper. "First to my fellow vervets: like the red tails and other monkeys, we also have limitless possibilities. Let us not be trapped by our past. It is unfortunate that many times we allow ourselves to be influenced by gibberish from monkeys who don't wish us well. Let us stop doing that. When you listen to something over and over, you begin to believe it and begin to live it. If you are listening to something good—great! But for many of us, we waste our time feeding our minds with negative input. Know that no one can change the pattern of your life unless you give them permission.

"We should learn to live by the rules and to live responsible lives. If we do, we will succeed. There are no shortcuts to success. The path is hard work. Look at the vervets who have made it in life. They did not do it sitting down. Their success was not by chance. They worked hard. Let it sink into our minds that the Maasai Mara provides opportunities for all of us.

"Talking of being responsible, I remember an incident that happened in Koiyaki. Our school had been given equipment to help us with our schoolwork, but one vervet monkey decided to smash all that equipment with a rock, just for fun.

"Some red-tailed monkeys saw him and called the principal, who was also a red-tailed monkey. When the vervet monkey realized that he had been seen, he tried to run away, but the school guard, who was also a red tail, chased after him and caught him. The school guard brought him back into the school building, and the principal came over and demanded an explanation for his poor behavior. The boy rudely said that he would report the principal to his mother and that his mother would then deal with the principal.

"The principal called the boy's mother, and when she arrived, he took her to the room where her son had broken the equipment. The principal told her the school could not tolerate such behavior and her son would be suspended. But she told him that that was not going to happen and that there was no way her son would be suspended. She began to curse the principal, telling him that her son was being victimized for being a vervet. She asked if her son was the first one to break things at the school. She wanted to know if red-tailed monkeys didn't also break things."

Sankey shook his head and scanned the class, looking at his fellow vervets. He said that with this kind of parent, vervet kids would go nowhere. "This kind of behavior from a parent is not helping the child. Children need to be disciplined when they have done something wrong. To defend children when they are in the wrong is to lead them down a path of destruction," he said. "The system may not be fair, but two wrongs don't make a right. You should not give monkeys who don't like you the opportunity not to respect you because of your unruly behavior."

Sankey told the class that the destructive monkey had not stayed in school and had tragically been killed in a fight a few months later.

Sankey emphasized to his fellow vervets that school was the only weapon they could use to change any unfairness in the system. Dropping out of school only strengthened those who didn't wish vervets well.

Pointing at the vervets in the class, Sankey asked them, "When the name *vervet* is mentioned, what mental picture comes into your mind? Do you see success, or do you see failure?"

No one responded. He pleaded with them to believe in the power of education to change their futures and to nurture positive mental pictures of themselves. "If you don't get some sort of education," Sankey said, "you will be a permanent underclass in the great Maasai Mara, a land of opportunities."

Turning to the red-tailed monkeys, Sankey said, "And to you, my red-tailed friends, let us learn to value each other. We should avoid statements that raise bitterness in each other. Such statements serve to widen the gap that has been planted in our minds by our parents. We are not born knowing the difference between vervets and red tails or any other kind of monkey. Prejudices are planted in our minds by our parents.

"Our being together here at school is our once-in-a-lifetime opportunity to learn how our differences can unite us. We are like the different musical instruments the Maasai people play.

"Our differences give us a rare opportunity to produce great harmony in the Maasai Mara. Forget the stories designed to destroy harmony. Let us blend together and be part of a great orchestra producing beautiful harmonies. Let us stop bringing discord to the song that forms the foundation of our blending together. Let us stop poisoning the fountain of our existence. There is no reason strong enough to make us keep souring our relationships. We need to bridge the gap.

"We don't want the tourists who come to visit our land—like our friends from the Serengeti—to be disappointed by our behavior. It does not matter whether you are a red tail, vervet, mantled guereza, or gibbon. We are all monkeys. I don't see myself as a vervet.

I see myself as a monkey. Together we can teach our parents. We should help them to know that we will accept the good lessons they give us but will treat the bad as junk."

Sankey looked at Miss Pam, and she nodded, encouraging him to go on.

He wiped his brow and said, "May I remind you that you are writing the script of your life for others to read. What do you want others to read about you? Let us all be well motivated and willing to learn from each other. Don't budget for failure. If, in the depths of your heart, you tell yourself that this is difficult and cannot be done, you are budgeting for failure. If you say, 'This is what our parents have always told us,' you are budgeting for failure. We are a new generation of monkeys. We should always plan to succeed. We should always be open minded and willing to accommodate new ways of thinking." Sankey then thanked the teacher for giving him a chance to speak and the class for giving him their undivided attention.

The class was awestruck. They had never seen such a vervet monkey. They had no choice but to put their hands together for him. As he walked to his seat, all eyes followed him. They could not believe that they had such a brilliant and positive-thinking vervet in their class.

Miss Pam could not believe it either. This was some vervet monkey. She thanked Sankey for his wise speech and then told the class that there was nothing else she could add. No one could have said it any better than one of their peers.

"I have never heard a vervet monkey speak like that," a jealous Punkey said, trying to shift the focus from Sankey. "I wonder if he is really a true vervet. He must have lots of red-tail blood in him," Punkey said sarcastically.

At that, Lankey leaped into the air and landed on the ground with a loud thump.

He shook his fist at Punkey and said, "Don't forget that I'm here! And you know me. If you have forgotten, let me remind you who I am. My name is Lankey! I will deal with you after class." With that he sat down.

"Miss Pam, may I say something?" Sankey looked calmly at the teacher, waiting to be given permission.

"Go ahead." Miss Pam nodded.

"I wish I knew the name of that friend of mine who doubts I am a genuine vervet," Sankey said evenly.

"My name is Punkey," Punkey shot back.

"Thank you, Punkey," Sankey said softly. "I am a genuine vervet. But what matters to me most is that I am a monkey." His face broke into a smile. "I would like to respect you and be your friend. I hope you will help me do that by having a little respect for me," Sankey said. "And for as for you, Lankey, fighting is the wrong way to settle issues. You cannot use your fists to fight your way to success. If you would like to silence people like Punkey and his red-tailed friends, the best way is to study hard and remain in school. Then later on, get a good job. That's the way to do it. I don't know how I will do in this school, but I have always worked hard and have been able to get good grades."

At recess that day, Sankey's classmates discovered that not only was he a good speaker and an A student, but he also was good at sports. And Sankey discovered that Punkey was excellent at sports too.

As they walked back to class after recess, Sankey went over to Punkey, shook his hand, and congratulated him on his sporting abilities. Punkey smiled and said that he admired Sankey as well. As they walked together, Punkey hesitantly apologized for what he had said in class. Sankey smiled and told him not to worry about it, as it was not his fault and all had to do with what his parents had told him about vervets. Sankey explained that this was their chance to break loose from the old way of thinking and create a new generation of monkeys.

As they entered the class, the students could tell that something had happened. Sankey, a vervet, and Punkey, a red tail, had clicked. Change was in the air.

After class, Sankey and Punkey sat on the ground and talked for a long time. Lankey hid behind a bush eavesdropping.

He could not figure out what was wrong with this vervet called Sankey.

Chapter 10

An Unexpected Outcome

SANKEY HAD BEEN IN THE area for a year when he and his mother and Lankey and his parents decided to enjoy a day together at the Mara River. Just as they were packing up to leave, they were startled by a cry for help coming from upstream. Way upriver they saw a monkey frantically waving his hands before disappearing under the water. After a short time, the monkey reappeared.

"That monkey is going to drown!" Sankey shouted.

"We must save him!" Lankey yelled, looking at his parents.

As the monkey was swept closer to them, Sankey exclaimed, "Hey, that looks like Punkey!"

Lankey squinted his eyes and looked carefully. Then, turning to his dad and mom, he said, "Sankey's right—it *is* Punkey. That's the guy who has been at the forefront of bullying us vervets at school." He paused and, looking defiant, said, "I think it's time he faced the music."

"I think so too!" Lankey's mom said in support.

"Nature has a way of punishing evil monkeys like Punkey," Lankey's dad said with a smile.

Sankey looked at them and quickly said, "I know it hurts when someone bullies you, but two wrongs don't make a right. What are we going to gain by letting him die? Revenge is for simpleminded people. To love those who bully and persecute you is a sign of greatness. It's the highest quality one can possess."

The three monkeys looked at each other, allowing Sankey's words to sink in.

"I have always taught my son to rise above the nonsense in life," Sankey's mom said. "A spirit of revenge keeps you at the level of your opponent. A spirit of revenge makes your enemy your equal. We must rise above that."

Lankey's parents looked ashamed. Then his mom said, "You are right. We should help him."

"Here he comes. Let's hurry!" Sankey said, looking at the group with renewed energy.

"Punkey needs our help, and we have no time to waste!" Lankey shouted.

"Lankey, quickly bring me that pole over there," Lankey's dad commanded with urgency in his voice.

Lankey got the pole, and his dad stretched it over the water, holding the other end tightly.

"I hope he will be able to grab it!" Sankey's mom said, wringing her hands.

Lankey shouted above the noise of the water, "Punkey! Grab the pole, and we'll pull you to safety!"

Punkey waved his hands in the air and again disappeared under the water.

"Where did he go?" Lankey asked frantically.

They all looked around, but Punkey was nowhere to be seen.

"What happened to him?" Sankey's mother asked, tears welling in her eyes.

They continued scanning the water. When Punkey finally reappeared, he had passed the pole and was going downstream.

"There he goes!" Lankey's mother shouted.

Lankey's dad, pulling the pole behind him, ran down parallel to the stream, Sankey and Lankey close behind him. The water thrust Punkey toward some rocks, and he got wedged between them. Lankey's dad, Sankey, and Lankey arrived at the bank of the river, panting like dogs that had been chasing a rabbit. A little later the two mothers arrived.

"Punkey, we're going to throw this pole out to you!" Lankey's dad shouted at the top of his voice.

"Okay!" called a trembling and tearful Punkey.

"Hold the end tight, and we'll pull you across!" Lankey's dad said.

"I'll try," Punkey replied. Then he looked carefully at the monkeys on the shore and asked, "Is that you, Lankey? And is that Sankey?"

"Yes," they answered in unison.

"We are going to save you, Punkey!" Lankey cried.

"And we have no time to waste," Lankey's dad said. He extended the pole out toward Punkey.

"I can't believe you're doing this for me," Punkey said, not believing what he was seeing or hearing.

"Quickly! Grab the pole—and hold it tight!" Sankey commanded.

Punkey stretched out his hands and grabbed the end of the pole. Sankey, Lankey, and Lankey's dad began to pull the terrified Punkey toward the riverbank. The mothers, their hearts beating like drums, watched apprehensively. Sometimes Punkey would disappear in the water's white foam and then reappear.

As the rescuers continued pulling Punkey to safety, he suddenly shouted, "My hands are getting tired! I'm slipping!"

"Hold on!" Sankey shouted. "Just hold on!"

"I'm losing my grip!" Punkey shouted as his left hand slipped from the pole.

"Don't give up!" Sankey's mom pleaded.

Punkey struggled to regain his grip on the pole, but slowly his right hand also began to slip.

"We're losing him!" Lankey's dad exclaimed.

"Just hold tight!" Lankey shouted.

Just when Punkey was about to reach the shore, the pole slipped out of his hand, and he disappeared into the white foam.

"Oh no! He's gone!" Lankey screamed.

Just then Punkey reappeared. Lankey dived into the water and grabbed the exhausted monkey before he could be swept away again.

"Be careful of crocodiles!" Lankey's mom shouted frantically.

Lankey's dad stretched out the pole, and Lankey grabbed it. With one hand he held on to Punkey, and with the other he held the pole until they were both pulled to safety.

Punkey, his teeth chattering from shock and fear, lay on his back on the bank of the river in a state of exhaustion. The other monkeys all knelt around him, their chests heaving up and down from tiredness and excitement. Punkey smiled faintly, not believing his luck.

Once everyone was rested, Punkey looked at Sankey, Lankey, and their parents, and tears began to flow down his face. In between sobs Punkey tried to say something. "Please … please …" He was choked with emotion and could not speak. Sankey and Lankey moved closer to him and reassured him that everything was okay—there was no need to worry.

After some time, Punkey said, "Please forgive me. If you had treated me the way I deserved, I would have died today." He wiped at the tears running down his face.

"Don't worry, Punkey. We love you and have no grudge against you," Lankey said. "To be honest with you, when I realized that it was you, I had no intention of helping you. I am ashamed to say that I wanted you to die. When I told my parents that you were the guy who bullied me and the other vervets at school, they didn't want to do anything to help you either. But Sankey and his mother"—Lankey looked at Sankey and his mother and then back at Punkey—"convinced us that we would not benefit at all from letting you die. They helped us understand that revenge is for simpleminded people."

"We are happy that you are alive," Lankey's mom said.

"I have learned a great lesson from Sankey and his mom," Lankey's dad said, rubbing his hands together.

"But I don't understand why you saved my life when I've made your lives so difficult at school!" Punkey said. "This was your opportunity as vervets to get revenge."

Nobody said anything for a while. Then Punkey said, "I don't understand why we treat each other the way we do. We are all monkeys, and there is no reason for us to hate each other so much." He looked thoughtful. "I wonder why we do the things we do to each other."

"It's anybody's guess," Sankey's mother said with a shrug.

After an awkward silence, Punkey said slowly, "I think I know why."

"What do you think is the reason?" Lankey asked.

"You know, Lankey, do you remember years ago when we used to play together?" Punkey asked.

"Yeah," Lankey replied.

"My parents were not happy that we were playing together. Whenever we began playing together, they would call my sister and me away."

"I remember that," Lankey said.

"They told my sister and me that you vervets are evil, that you are criminals, and that playing with you would spoil our good morals." Punkey shook his head dejectedly.

"I can't believe you're saying this! My parents also didn't like us playing together." Lankey turned to look at his mom and dad. "They told me that you red tails are proud and are to be avoided. They said that, since red tails don't respect vervets, I shouldn't waste my time with you guys."

Lankey's parents looked at Lankey and then at Sankey and his mom as they laughed uneasily.

"Now do you see where the mistrust comes from?" Punkey asked, his eyes solemn.

"Yep. When we were young, we had no problem playing together—until our parents began planting seeds of mistrust in us!" Lankey looked upset.

"When we are born, we don't know whether we are vervets or red tails until our parents begin to feed us all kinds of information about each other." Punkey shook his head regretfully.

"Punkey," Sankey said, "for me, though I am a vervet monkey, I have nothing against red-tailed monkeys. As I have said over and over, I see myself as a monkey and nothing else. I feel sad when others see me only as a vervet and not as a monkey." Sankey stood a bit taller and said passionately, "We all belong to the Maasai Mara."

As the monkeys began making their way home, Punkey said, "I have learned a big lesson today. You could have left me to die, but you chose to save me, a red-tailed monkey who did not deserve to be saved. At least, not by you." He kept silent for some time before saying, "Are you really willing to forgive me?"

Lankey smiled and said, "The fact that we decided to save you shows that we already forgave you." Lankey, Punkey, and Sankey shook hands and hugged each other.

Punkey took a deep breath and said, "Now that I have firsthand knowledge of you guys, my view of vervets has changed completely."

This experience marked a turning point for Punkey. From then on he had great respect for vervet monkeys. He was willing to do anything for them. The idea that his parents had planted in him that vervets were inferior began to disappear.

When Punkey arrived home, he told his parents how the vervets had saved him. He and his parents decided to go and thank Sankey and his mom and Lankey and his parents. As time went by, these three families became great friends.

At school, Punkey told everybody about what had happened over the weekend. He said that if it had not been for Sankey, Lankey, and their parents, he would have died in the Mara River. Punkey eloquently begged everyone to stop placing labels on others just because other monkeys were different from them.

In the days following, Punkey began to advocate for equality between vervets and red-tailed monkeys. Together with Shulley, Lankey, and Sankey, he formed the Fairness and Equality for All organization at school. Miss Pam and the principal were very pleased. One day during assembly, the principal told the students that she was very happy with the turn of events. She was happy that the students had started a movement that she believed would positively impact not only her school but the entire Maasai Mara.

Chapter 11

A Small Story That Brought about a Big Change

LANKEY'S PROBLEM OF GIVING UP and getting frustrated when things got difficult bothered his parents a great deal. Though they had talked to him many times already, they once again sat him down and tried to talk sense into him.

"There is no use trying," Lankey argued. "School is just so hard, and I'm wasting my time trying." With that, Lankey stormed away.

His parents decided to call Grandma, who lived up the Mara River, to come over and help. She arrived while Lankey was in school. "What's going on?" Grandma asked as soon as she had sat down. Mom and Dad told her to eat first and then they would tell her what was bothering them. But she replied that she would not enjoy her meal if she did not know why she had been called.

"Okay," Mom said, "we will tell you so that your heart can be settled."

They told her that although Lankey was an extremely gifted boy with many talents and was capable of getting Bs and even As, he did not want to try hard enough. He had come to believe that because he was a vervet, he could not do well. He had even told his parents that he would drop out of school altogether if they kept pushing him.

They told Grandma that on several occasions they had asked him to explain what was going on in his mind when he received Ds and Cs when he had demonstrated the ability to get As. His reply was that they should just accept him the way he was. Lankey's parents were at their wits' end, having done all they could to help him overcome this hurdle but without much success. Grandmother listened very carefully and told them that she would see what she could do.

When Lankey returned home from school, he was elated to see Grandmother. He put his books down, rushed over, and hugged her tightly. Thrilled and smiling from ear to ear, Grandma kissed her grandson.

Lankey loved it when Grandma came over because she always had lots of stories. Sure enough, after enjoying a hearty evening meal, Grandma gathered the family around her for story time.

She smiled, cleared her throat, and said, "I am so happy to see all of you again. I'm always happy when I come here to be with you, my family. Before we go to bed, I would like to tell you a story." She patted Punkey's head and began her story.

"There was a time when your grandfather and I had many rats in our home. After trying everything under the sun to eradicate these little monsters and failing every time, your grandfather and I decided to go see our family friends who lived near the Serengeti and ask for a cat. They had many cats; in fact, the first time we visited them we thought they had a zoo for cats!"

Grandma stopped and scanned the faces to see if her loved ones were all listening. Lankey begged her to go on. She smiled and said, "Getting a cat was a big sacrifice for me, considering that I'm allergic to cats. But something happened that made me decide that it was better to have allergy attacks than to have rats in my home.

"It happened one day just after lunch. I was taking a little nap when I suddenly woke up to something biting my toe. I quickly pulled my leg toward myself and sat up. I looked around but saw nothing. Wondering what was going on, I took a deep breath and went back to sleep. After a short time, I felt the biting again—this time more painful than the first. Completely shaken, I sat up just in time to see a rat scampering away. My toe was bleeding, and I feared that I could get rabies.

"I guess when you're tired, you're tired. So I dozed off again. Before too long, I felt something moving on my face. I instinctively reached for the thing and felt something soft in my hand. I quickly threw it away. It was a big rat. And when I say big, I mean big! I think it may even have been pregnant."

Grandma shivered and said, "To say that I was scared is an understatement. My face and palms were sweating, and my heart was beating like mad."

Her listeners chuckled nervously, their hearts racing as if the incident had happened to them.

"If I were to tell you of all the places we found rats," Grandma said, rubbing her hands together, "I would never finish this story. I must talk about the cat and not the rats. So let me get back to the cat.

"To get to our friends' home we had to go far up the Mara River, to a place where the river is a little narrower and there are lots of trees on both sides of the river, forming a little tree bridge across the river.

"We had to climb up one of the trees, swing from branch to branch, and then jump across the river to a tree on the other side. Then we could proceed with our journey, which consisted of many hours of walking.

"We arrived late in the evening and were exhausted. After eating a meal with our friends, we told them that we should be getting back. They tried to persuade us to spend the night and leave in the morning since it was already late and very dark, but we had done our research and had learned that cats should be transported at night so that they don't know where they have been taken to. Our friends saw the sense in this and gave us our new cat. It was black with a white patch on its forehead. We put it in a bag and tied the bag so that it would not be able to see where we were going. Your grandfather tied the bag to his back, and after thanking our friends for their hospitality and help, we headed out into the darkness on our way home. We walked with energy, knowing that the rats would soon be history. We arrived home in the early hours of the next morning. It was still dark, and everything was quiet.

"Your grandfather tied the cat to a big rock using a long rope so that it wouldn't be able to run away but would still have some freedom to move and reach its food and water. But he must not have tied the rope properly, because as we prepared to go to sleep, the cat managed to free itself and run away. We tried to run after it, but it disappeared into the darkness. We looked at each other, feeling very downhearted.

"Suddenly we heard a terrifying growl, then a loud meow, and then all was silent. We looked in the direction where the noises had come from. Our hearts sank because we were certain that the cat had been caught by some animal.

"We were so discouraged. We had spent most of the afternoon walking to our friends' home and most of the night walking back, and after all of this, we had nothing to show for it. When the sun arose, we went in the direction the growl had come from, and after some searching, we found the place where the cat had been attacked. There was blood on the grass. We felt terrible that the cat's life had ended this way. We regretted going to get it.

"Then your grandfather walked all the way back to our friends' place to tell them what had happened. When he returned later that afternoon, he brought with him another cat, which we managed to secure properly. This cat caught a lot of rats, and we were pleased with the job it was doing. But the fact that the other cat had been eaten by some animal kept bothering us.

"A week later, while sitting under our favorite tree, we saw our friends approaching from a distance. As soon as they saw us, they waved excitedly with big smiles on their faces. 'What a pleasant surprise!' we said to ourselves. But they had an even bigger surprise for us. As they came closer, we noticed that one friend had a bag tied around her belly.

"As soon as they arrived and sat down, they broke into laughter as our friend untied the bag from her belly to reveal what she had been carrying. It was the cat that had run away from us the week before! We could not believe our eyes. My friend explained that she and her children were on the veranda eating lunch when they heard a meowing coming from behind a corner of the cave. At first they did not pay any attention to it, because, after all, they had so many cats. But after a short time the cat came out from behind the corner, and it was the same black cat with a white patch on its forehead that had run away from us! It was thin and pale and looked very hungry. They could not believe their eyes. They gave it food, and it ate to its heart's content. It was limping, as one leg had been chewed away. It must have lost the leg when it was attacked soon after running away.

"I took the cat from my friend and held it firmly. I wondered how, with just three legs, it had been able to trace its way back to its home. It had taken six days of pain, but the cat had persevered and pressed on until it had made its way back to its final destination."

They all gave a sigh of relief, and Grandma said, "No one can deny that this cat had great determination. Though we cannot know for sure what it experienced as it navigated its way back home, it would not be far-fetched to imagine that it escaped a lot of dangers. Its thin, bloodstained body and three-legged limp told the whole story. Yet it was determined to find its way back home."

Lankey rubbed his eyes while Grandma continued, "Determination in life is very important. If this cat had given up, it would not have made it. In life, we should all learn to be determined no matter the circumstances. Giving up gets us nowhere. We should keep pushing on. There is always room for those who work hard. Though life is not always fair, you can never go wrong if you work hard."

Lankey reached up and shook Grandma's hand. "That's a great story, Grandma!" he said. "I have been inspired by this cat."

Mom and Dad had smiles on their faces. Then, as Grandma stroked his fur, Lankey asked, "Grandma, did Mom and Dad call you to come and give me a pep talk?" They all laughed as Grandma hugged him.

"You know, Lankey," Grandma said, "you may have big muscles, and that's good. But the only way to outdo the red tails is by reading, studying, and getting good grades."

Lankey flexed his muscles and, pointing at his head, said, "Muscles can't do it, but brains can!" Suddenly looking downcast, he said, "You know what, Grandma? I want to do well, but those red tails in my class keep laughing at me no matter what I do. When I get an A, they tell me that I'm wasting my time because no one trusts vervets anyway. I don't have the right color fur to make it in life. When I get a D, they still laugh at me and tell me that with such grades I will go nowhere in life!" Tears welled in Lankey's eyes as he said, "In my heart I want to do well, but the circumstances around me do not encourage me to succeed."

Grandma moved close to Lankey and wiped the tears from his face as she said, "The red tails say that because they want you to give up. Remember that we are survivors. We have gone through a lot as a group of monkeys. What we have gone through in the past is much worse than what we are going through now." Grandma looked into Lankey's eyes. "Don't play into the hands of those who don't wish you well. Rise above the nonsense of your detractors and know that, no matter how unfair things might be, we can make it. Look around you! You will see that there are a number of vervets who have made it. They met the same circumstances you are meeting, but they were determined to work against the odds and succeed. And they did!"

Lankey nodded in agreement. Mom said, "Many of the laws work against us, making us angry and sometimes afraid.

"But the only way to overcome this is to have the determination to move on, work hard, and remain in school. Do your best to avoid having arguments with MPF officers, because once they record you in their books, it can affect your whole future. Remain calm when provoked and try as best as you can to be polite. This is what your dad has done over the years."

Mom paused a moment and then said, "We are not telling you to be foolish but teaching you to be wise."

"And remember that not all MPF officers are bad. Many of them are very good." Grandma smiled at Lankey.

"And avoid bad friends," Dad chipped in. "Choose friends like Sankey instead."

"Who is Sankey?" Grandma asked curiously.

"Sankey is my classmate and is also a vervet. But he is different." Lankey paused for a moment and then said, "I guess Sankey has the spirit and determination of the cat Grandma just told us about. If the cat can do it and Sankey can do it, why not me?"

Lankey did not want to be outdone by a cat. Pretty soon he began to score Bs and even some As.

Chapter 12

Punkey Goes on Vacation

DURING SCHOOL VACATION IN AUGUST, Punkey and Shulley and their parents went to visit family friends who lived some distance away across the Mara River. In order to cross the river they had to use the same tree bridge that Lankey's grandparents had used when they'd gone to fetch the cat from their friends.

The family had planned to be with their friends for two weeks. The family friends had a boy who was around Punkey's age. Though it was the first time these two boys had met, they got along very well and were thrilled to be in each other's company. The second day they were there, the boy took Punkey to his room as the parents busied themselves with adult talk. He didn't tell his parents or Punkey's parents what he was planning to do.

About a week into their visit, Punkey's parents began to notice some strange behavior from Punkey. The two boys were spending long hours in the friend's room, and no one really knew what went on in there. This began to worry Punkey's parents.

One day, while Punkey and his friend were in the friend's room, the worried parents wondered if these secret meetings had anything to do with a certain root powder that the kids of the day were using. They talked of the dangers of the powder and how a number of kids had had their brains totally destroyed by it. The fathers decided it was time to investigate what was going on in that room.

When they knocked, it took some time for Punkey and his friend to respond. The parents could hear hurried noises and movements from inside the room, indicating that the boys must be hiding something. Eventually the dads were allowed in.

The boys looked nervous.

"What's going on, guys?" Punkey's friend's dad asked.

"Nothing!" the boy answered abruptly.

"So what is it that I smell in here?" his father pressed.

"Punkey!" Punkey's dad looked straight into Punkey's eyes. "What's going on?"

"What do you mean, Dad? We've just been hanging out!" Punkey said, looking as innocent as innocent can be.

"But what have you been doing?" his dad asked, raising his voice.

Punkey looked startled. "I told you we've been doing nothing! But since you seem to think that we've been doing something, why don't you tell us?" Even Punkey was surprised at his disrespect.

"Boys," Punkey's friend's dad said, "if you have been using that root powder, you are headed for trouble. It is illegal. Apart from landing yourself in big trouble with the authorities and us, your parents, it will destroy your brains, and you will be out of school, walking the streets of Maasai Mara."

Punkey and his friend looked down and then at their parents and said nothing. The parents marched out.

"That was close!" Punkey's friend said as he lifted a rock, revealing the powder.

Punkey looked at his friend and said, "A friend of mine from school, Sankey, told us that his dad was killed by a leopard because he was under the influence of this powder. Can that really happen?"

His friend laughed. "Have you not enjoyed the powder?"

"I have! It's great!" Punkey enthused.

"So why worry about some dead monkey when you are alive and enjoying the powder?" His friend did a little monkey jive and continued to sniff the powder.

Anxiously Punkey asked, "Where can I find the powder when I return home?"

"There are many places," his friend said. He explained where Punkey could get the powder and what to do so that he would not get caught. He also told Punkey that he would give him some for the journey home. He warned Punkey to be careful because, should the MPF get him, he would be in a great deal of trouble.

Punkey Risks His Life

Punkey's parents were relieved when the two weeks were over and the family could head home. On the day they left, Punkey was acting strange. When his parents asked him if he was okay, all he said was that he was excited that they were going back home. Although they seemed to be satisfied with the answer, a shadow of doubt remained on their faces.

They walked for some time. As they neared the tree bridge, suddenly Dad stopped. "Listen!" he said. "What's that thundering noise?"

The monkeys stopped and listened. What they heard was the sound of thousands of hooves beating the earth. The great migration was taking place! The wildebeests were migrating from the Serengeti to the Maasai Mara. "Welcome home!" Shulley shouted. They all watched in awe as the magnificent beasts headed for the river.

Punkey's adventurous and curious nature, in combination with the powder working in his system, brought a naughty smile to his lips. His feverish mind began to brew a novel thought. Wouldn't it be so much more fun to ride on the back of one of the wildebeests as it crossed the river than to use the tree bridge? But how was he going to prevent his family from stopping him?

His heart beat faster and faster as they neared the bridge. Suddenly, an idea popped into his mind. He asked his dad if he could go and attend to the call of nature.

"No problem," his dad said. "We'll go ahead and cross the river, and you can find us on the other side when you're done."

Punkey was thrilled. He did not stop to think what his parents' reaction would be when they saw him risking life and limb crossing the crocodile-infested Mara River on the back of a wildebeest. He also did not consider what his fate would be if the wildebeest he was riding should be grabbed by a crocodile. He simply ran as fast as he could toward the oncoming wildebeests, filled with both excitement and fear.

After reaching the other side of the river, Punkey's family waited patiently for him to join them. Five minutes went by, then another five. Punkey was nowhere to be seen. The family decided to slowly continue their journey along the edge of the Mara River, convinced that Punkey would soon catch up with them. But just as they were about to set off, they heard a loud shout.

Turning back toward the river, they could not believe what their eyes were seeing. Punkey was excitedly waving his hands as he rode on the back of a wildebeest toward the river.

"Get down from there!" Dad shouted as more and more wildebeests splashed into the river.

The family ran toward where the animals were crossing. As they got nearer, what they saw gave them chills. Crocodiles that had been hiding beneath the water began to attack the herd of wildebeests from all sides. Frantic victims were caught in the strong jaws of the reptiles and pulled under the water.

The helpless family watched from the riverbank as Punkey's wildebeest leaped into the water with a big splash.

Then it happened. A huge crocodile lunged out of the water toward the wildebeest that Punkey was riding. It sank its teeth into the wildebeest's side, catching Punkey's foot in the process. Terrified, Punkey screamed as the crocodile began to drag the wildebeest down into the water. He managed to free his leg, but he was badly injured.

Just then, Punkey was hit by another wildebeest as the animal vigorously pushed itself toward the riverbank. Screaming, he found himself flying up into the air. Luckily for Punkey, when he came down, he landed on the back of the wildebeest and was carried up onto the riverbank. When the wildebeest shook its body to dry itself, Punkey was thrown off its back and landed on the ground like a floppy ragdoll, his right leg bleeding profusely.

Punkey's family rushed to his side. He was very much shaken but thankful to be alive. His father picked him up and carried him out of the path of the stampeding animals and then gently put him down to inspect his injured leg. It was in bad shape, the skin torn and bleeding, but fortunately there were no bones broken. Shulley shook her head, not understanding why her brother did such crazy things.

After the initial shock had subsided, Punkey's parents, both shaken and angry, demanded an explanation for his dishonesty and recklessness. "You could have died!" his mother chided.

At first, Punkey was silent and ashamed, but after a while he was able to give his family a reason for his poor judgment. He told his parents how his friend had introduced him to the root powder, which provided a pleasurable sensation, like a rush of energy, and which seemed to remove all fear from him. "It was this root powder that caused us to keep to ourselves most of the time," he confessed. "Just before we left to return home, I used some. I think that's what made me so careless." Big tears rolled down Punkey's face. "I will never use that root again!"

His mother's face softened as she hugged him close. "Son, the consequences of lying can be destructive. Your lies will always find you out."

Punkey nodded in agreement.

His dad cleared his throat and said, "We are happy you have said it yourself that you will not use that root again."

Again, Punkey nodded.

"You could have died, Punkey!" Shulley shivered. "I don't want to lose my brother. I love you!" she exclaimed as she helped him stand up. After making sure that he could walk despite the pain, Punkey's family slowly headed home.

It would have been great if Punkey really had learned his lesson. It would have been great if Punkey had really learned that what is fun and enjoyable is not always good for you. And it would have been great if Punkey had really learned that it is good to always tell the truth. But unfortunately, this was not the case.

Chapter 13

Punkey and Lankey Get Caught in the Maasai People's Pots

THOUGH MANY OF THE MAASAI people's inkajijiks were built inside enkangs, it was not unusual to see some inkajijiks dotted outside an enkang. This was the case for a frustrated Maasai woman who had noticed that her things kept going missing. One day she complained to her husband, saying she did not know what was going on.

If she left peanuts in a basket, when she came back, they would be gone. If she put down some food to go inside to fetch water, when she got back, the food would be gone. All sorts of things had disappeared.

Her husband listened carefully as she poured out her frustrations. He scratched his head, thought for a while, and then told her that he would visit the village elder, who was known for his wise advice. He assured her that the culprit would be found.

The elder's inkajijik stood alone some distance away from the other inkajijiks. The man told the elder what his wife had told him. The wise man listened carefully. When the man finished speaking, the elder smiled. He told the man that he knew what was going on and gave a detailed explanation of what to do. Smiling, the husband thanked the wise man and hurried home.

Excitement written all over his face, he bounded into his inkajijik bellowing his wife's name at the top of his voice. His surprised wife stopped what she was doing as her husband told her she should make three big clay pots. "The mouths of two of the pots should be very small, so that if a monkey made a fist inside the pot, it would not be able to pull it out," he said. "The other pot should have a normal mouth, such that a monkey could pull its fist out."

The woman quickly went to work. She molded the pots and dried them in the sun. Then she baked them in a big fire until they were properly hardened. If you hit them gently, they sounded like musical instruments.

The man thanked his wife for a job well done. Then, as his wife and children watched, he filled each pot halfway with peanuts and placed them outside, behind the hut. He told his family to occasionally dip their hands into the pot with the big mouth, take some peanuts, and eat them. They did this for about three days.

Punkey, Lankey, and Sankey Visit the Maasai village

When Punkey returned from his vacation, Lankey and Sankey were thrilled to have him back. Sitting in their favorite tree, they talked excitedly about everything they had done during the school break and caught up on all the news. Punkey told them how he had almost been caught by a crocodile in the Mara River after riding on the back of a wildebeest. His friends could not believe that he had actually done such a daring thing. "We are glad to see you alive and in one piece!" said a smiling Sankey.

Suddenly Punkey began to rub his hands together and look around to see if there was anyone nearby. He lowered his voice and told his friends how he and his new friend had enjoyed sniffing a certain root powder. He told them that he had never felt anything as exhilarating. He said that he knew that some guys at school were using it.

He smiled as he pulled something from his pocket. "I have some of it here," he whispered, unrolling a leaf while continuing to scan their surroundings. He placed the unrolled leaf on his open palm, revealing a brownish powder. He looked at Lankey and Sankey to see if they approved. Neither of his friends said a thing.

He took a deep breath and said, "Here is how you use it." He put his nose close to the powder and sniffed. Sneezing and wiping tears from his eyes with the back of his other hand, he smiled and offered the stuff to his friends. Sankey and Lankey looked at each other and then at him. "It's good!" Punkey assured them as he sniffed some more. "Try it!"

Lankey looked at Sankey and then reached for the stuff and sniffed some. But Sankey refused. He reminded them what he had told them the first day he'd come to class—that his father had died because of that powder.

"Your dad didn't die from using this stuff—a leopard killed him!" Punkey mockingly interjected.

"And your dad was probably old and couldn't run," Lankey chipped in, rolling his eyes mischievously.

Sankey looked at them and said, "You can say that my father was old, but sniffing that stuff has the same end result—death. I made up my mind not to mess with it when I saw how my father died. It was a very foolish death." He shook his head to emphasize his decision.

As Punkey and Lankey continued to sniff the powder, Sankey tried to convince them that they were putting their lives in danger. Lankey smiled and said, "Most guys at school have used it at one time or another. And some of them use it regularly, and they're all still alive." Lankey looked at Sankey and added, "And most of them get good grades too." But Sankey was unmoved.

After some minutes, Lankey began to leap from branch to branch, shouting, "I'm feeling bigger and better! I feel like I could even kill a leopard!" He didn't seem to care that doing somersaults so high up in the branches was dangerous.

Sankey remained calm, though he knew that Lankey was trying to insult him.

Then Punkey jumped from the tree, whizzed through the air, and landed on the ground. He looked up at his friends. "Monkey-body technology has defied the laws of gravity and has landed safely!" he said triumphantly, his voice filled with excitement. Lankey clapped and cheered as Punkey climbed back to where his friends were.

They heard singing coming from the Maasai village and decided to go and check it out. When they neared the village, they climbed a tree and looked out over the valley to discover the cause of the excitement. All the Maasai people were outside the fence and were dancing, entertaining the tourists who were visiting the village.

Suddenly, Lankey noticed three clay pots behind one of the inkajijik outside the enkang. He pointed them out to his friends. They watched as first a Maasai man and then a woman left the dancers and walked over to the pots. They each took out some peanuts, cracked the shells, and ate the yummy delicacy. The couple did this several times. The three monkeys looked at each other, hardly able to comprehend how there could be so many peanuts in the pots. Eventually the dancers, including the couple, walked away, leading the tourists to the kraals where the cattle were kept. An excited Punkey suggested that they go and take some peanuts for themselves. Lankey agreed, but Sankey said that the whole thing looked very suspicious.

"What do you mean 'suspicious'?" Punkey shot back.

"Why are those three pots outside the inkajijik?" Sankey asked.

"If you had sniffed the powder, you wouldn't be thinking that way. You wouldn't be such a coward!" Lankey teased.

"Whatever you say, I'm not going." Sankey was adamant.

Without a moment's hesitation, Punkey and Lankey climbed down the tree and dashed for the pot with the big mouth. They fished out some peanuts and enjoyed them. Soon they had finished the peanuts in this pot.

They dashed for the two narrow-mouthed pots, Punkey heading for one and Lankey for the other. They squeezed their hands into the pots and scooped up great big handfuls of peanuts. But when they tried to pull their hands out, they found that their hands were stuck inside!

The foolish monkeys struggled to free themselves. They could not reason that all they needed to do to free their hands was to let go of the peanuts. The pots were too big and heavy for them to run away carrying the pots with them. They wiggled, twisted, and turned their trapped hands but failed to free themselves. They shrieked in desperation. Sankey quickly came down and tried to free them, but he also failed.

All of a sudden, the Maasai husband appeared. When Sankey saw him, he looked at his friends as if to say, *Sorry, brothers, but I'm outta here!* He then dashed off and scampered up a tree some distance away.

The visibly angry Maasai man grabbed Punkey and broke the pot. Shaking Punkey violently, the man said, "Today, you are going to die." He tied Punkey's feet and hands with a rope and threw him to the ground. He then grabbed Lankey and shook him too, but as he tried to tie him up, somehow Lankey managed to bite the man's hand. The man screamed in pain and threw Lankey down. Lankey took off for dear life, the man chasing close behind.

As Lankey staggered up a nearby tree, the effects of the root powder caused him to slip and fall right into the hands of the Maasai man. The man tightened his grip on the frightened monkey, but Lankey scratched the man's face. Again the Maasai man screamed and dropped him. Blood gushed from the cuts on his face. Lankey managed to run to the tree where Sankey was and haul himself to safety.

"I will get you next time!" the man shouted as he angrily walked back to where Punkey was tied up. He wiped the blood off his face and picked up Punkey. "So *you* are the one who has been stealing my wife's things! Today we will fix you!" He grabbed a large knife from his hut.

Poor Punkey! He had just returned home from vacation and hadn't even known that things were being stolen from this Maasai family. His father and mother back home had no idea what was happening to him in the Maasai village. There he was—trapped and not knowing what would happen to him.

Just then, the man's wife appeared. When she saw Punkey in her husband's hands, she danced and clapped her hands. Punkey wailed, undoubtedly begging for his life.

Fearing that Punkey was about to be killed, Lankey and Sankey took off to go get help. Lankey, still weak from the root powder, struggled to keep pace with Sankey.

"I told you not to use that powder!" Sankey reproached. "It's affected you greatly."

All Lankey could do was nod in shame.

"You made fun of how my dad died, but if a leopard came now, just like my dad, you would be dead meat," Sankey said.

Again, all Lankey could do was nod in agreement as he huffed and puffed, trying to keep up with Sankey.

Punkey Meets His Fate

With a knife in his right hand and his family following close behind, the Maasai man took Punkey to the wise man.

The wise man was seated on his veranda. When he saw Punkey, a smile of satisfaction spread across his face. He took Punkey in his hands, looked at him for some time, and then handed him back to the Maasai man.

Telling the man to wait on the veranda, he quickly disappeared into the hut. When he came back out, he had in his hands a cloth that had been made to look like a leopard skin. It looked very realistic. The old man sat down and asked for Punkey. The puzzled family looked at each other, wondering what the wise man was up to.

The old man explained that he was going to sew the leopard cloth onto Punkey, covering him completely so that he would look like a leopard. He would then muzzle Punkey's mouth so that he could not make monkey sounds and let him go. The old man said, "Monkeys fear leopards, so when the other monkeys see him coming, they will run away, thinking that it is a leopard coming after them. But this monkey will continue running after his fellow monkeys so that they can help him get rid of the leopard cloth. And so he will end up chasing the monkeys far away from our village!"

The Maasai couple and their children all looked at each other and smiled. "You are very wise," the husband said, looking very happy.

"You're a genius!" the wife added, looking very satisfied with the plan.

The wise man started sewing the cloth onto Punkey's body. "They don't call me wise for nothing," he said as he continued with his work.

He sewed the cloth around Punkey so tightly that there was no way Punkey would be able to get it off on his own.

Sankey and Lankey Report Punkey's Fate

Punkey's two friends finally arrived at his parents' place and reported what had happened. Terrified by the news, Punkey's parents, Sankey, and Shulley, with a huffing and puffing Lankey close behind them, dashed to the monkey chief's residence. When they arrived at the compound, they were all out of breath, but Lankey had suffered much more than the others from all the running. He needed to sit down immediately, as he felt extremely tired, and he looked quite confused.

The chief's place was very beautiful. His caves were surrounded by lots of bushy green trees that were used for shelter when it was very hot. Some distance from the chief's official residence stood a big tree with spreading branches that provided good shade. Many monkeys could sit under the tree. In fact, the monkeys used it as their court, to settle disputes among themselves. Not far from the chief's place was the Mara River. From up in the tree the monkeys could see hippos and crocodiles swimming in the river. Early in the mornings and in the evenings, they could see lots of animals that came to drink from the Mara River.

Past the big, umbrella-like tree, between the Mara River and the chief's place, was a large open area with lots of rocks and trees and a large anthill right in the center. When the chief received official visitors from the many parts of the Maasai Mara, the Serengeti, and other distant places, this open area was where they enjoyed all kinds of activities.

When the chief learned from Punkey's parents what had happened, he commanded one of his messengers to blow the summoning horn. In no time at all, the MPF as well as the specialized group of monkeys known as the Eight Scorpions, or the 8S, came running, ready for war.

The chief briefed them about what had happened and then told them that it was their duty to go and search for Punkey. As the MPF and the 8S organized themselves, the messenger blew his horn again, and many monkeys came. The chief told them that Punkey had been captured by the Maasai people for stealing peanuts and that the last thing his friends had seen was a Maasai man about to cut Punkey's throat.

Punkey's mother and sister were heartbroken. Close friends of Punkey and his family began to sob, and his schoolmates and teachers all looked very sad. The chief cleared his throat and said, "We don't know what state Punkey is in now. We trust that our professional teams will be able to rescue our young friend."

The leader of the 8S called the leader of the MPF aside, and the two discussed something together before walking over to the chief. The leader of the MPF whispered something into the chief's ear, and the chief nodded in approval. Then the MPF leader said to the crowd of monkeys, "My fellow monkeys, the members of the MPF and the 8S are seasoned and professional warriors. We will do our best to find Punkey." He paused for a moment, took a deep breath, and said, "If we do not find him alive, we will do our best to find his body so that he can have a decent burial."

The chief nodded again in approval, cleared his throat, and then barked, "All the other monkeys should remain here until the MPF and the 8S return." With that the chief shook hands with the leaders of the MPF and the 8S and wished them good luck.

Punkey's dad asked to join the MPF. "I have to go and find my son," he sobbed. The leader of the MPF agreed to let him come.

The group started off on the search. The two leaders asked Sankey and Lankey to show them to the place they had last seen their friend. As they started to walk, it became clear that Lankey was not himself. The MPF and the 8S soon discovered that he had used the root powder, and they left him in the chief's hands to be dealt with. It was now up to Sankey alone to guide the group.

Punkey Is Released

When the wise man was done sewing the leopard-skin cloth on Punkey's body, all the people laughed. Punkey looked just like a leopard. The wise man lifted him up and said, "This is your punishment for stealing our things." With that, he took hold of Punkey's hind legs, swung him around several times, and let him go. Punkey flew through the air for what seemed to him like an eternity before landing on the ground with a loud thud some distance away from the wise man's inkajijik. Dazed, Punkey stood up and walked unsteadily forward as he tried to regain his balance. When his senses finally came together, he began to run. But, just like Lankey, the root powder was still affecting him, making him unsteady on his feet. Nevertheless, he ran as fast as his legs would carry him.

Punkey could not believe his luck to have escaped with his life. But as he looked at the leopard-skin cloth sewn around his body, he realized that no monkey would want to be near him, because he now looked just like a leopard. Feeling discouraged, he made his way toward home. As he jumped from tree to tree, he hoped that someone would recognize him despite his changed appearance.

The MPF Meet a "Leopard"

The MPF and the 8S decided to split up. They called Punkey's name as they searched, but there was no response. After a long time of searching with no success, many gave up hope. Punkey's father was very sad. He did not know how his wife was going to take this news.

All of a sudden, a few of the monkeys in the MPF spotted a "leopard" coming their way. In a flash, chaos enveloped the scene as terrified and barking monkeys ran in every direction to save their lives. Using every ounce of their energy and every fiber of their muscles, the monkeys ran for their lives.

It had not taken long for Punkey to recognize his father and Sankey, but recognizing them did not help him in any way. He could not bark, because his mouth was partly muzzled. He ran after the monkeys in the hope that someone would recognize him, but he could not keep up with them. Soon, all the monkeys were gone.

Poor Punkey! Tired, lonely, and very much afraid, he sat on a branch, tears rolling down his cheeks.

After some time, the scattered monkeys regrouped back at the chief's place. The 8S was already there, having given up the search. The MPF leader told the chief about the "leopard" that had chased them and almost even caught some of them. The chief and the people listened, wondering where the leopard was now. The monkeys cast wary glances all around.

Punkey's mother tearfully pleaded with the MPF to make one more attempt. Punkey's dad and Shulley came and stood by her as she made her desperate appeals. "Please help me find my son!" she sobbed. Her husband rubbed her head, and Shulley held her hand as tears flowed down all their cheeks. Punkey's mother said, "I would rather die than to leave this place without my son."

Everyone was silent. The chief looked at Punkey's family, at the MPF, and then at all the monkeys. He ran his hand slowly through the fur of his head. Just as he opened his mouth to speak, in the distance the monkeys spotted a "leopard" wobbling toward them.

The monkeys screamed and took off in all directions. The chief and his family disappeared into the thicket of bushy leaves. Everybody ran away except for Punkey's mother. She just sat there and cried, "I would rather die than leave this place without my son!"

Punkey saw his mother and wobbled toward her. The monkeys screamed for Punkey's mom to run away, but she refused to leave. Punkey gathered his courage and ran faster and faster toward his mother. Too depressed to do anything, she just sat there and looked at the leopard as it approached.

When Punkey's father saw what was going on, he turned back to go and rescue his wife. Some of the 8S also came running. Punkey leaped on his mother and hugged her tight. Punkey's father grabbed the "leopard" by the scruff of its neck and tried to pull it away from his wife, but it held tight. The 8S pushed Punkey's father away. Three 8S guys grabbed the "leopard," and their leader shouted, "One, two, three, pull!" They all yanked hard on the "leopard's" skin, trying to get the creature away from Punkey's mother. To everybody's amazement, the "leopard's" skin came right off!

Punkey's father gasped as he realized that the "leopard" was actually Punkey. "Punkey!" he yelled with glee.

Punkey cried and held his mother tight. A few of the scattered monkeys drifted back to the scene. They could not believe what they were seeing. For sure, it was Punkey! Realizing that the leopard was not a real leopard at all, the rest of the monkeys all ran back to see what this leopard business was all about.

The chief joined the happy and confused group. As the monkeys talked to Punkey, they quickly realized that Punkey, like Lankey, had used the root powder.

The visibly angry chief, the leader of the MPF, and many of the red-tailed monkeys demanded to know why Punkey, a red-tailed monkey, would be using stuff that was mostly used by vervets.

"We could have lost our son because of the bad behavior of vervets!" the chief lamented. "We've always told you to avoid those vervets!" Punkey's father said angrily to Punkey.

Shocked, Sankey looked at the chief, then at the leader of the MPF, then at Punkey's father, and then at Punkey. He was incredulous that the red tails would so quickly arrive at the conclusion that it was vervets who had misled Punkey.

Punkey just shook his head because he knew the thinking of the red-tailed monkeys, although he wished that someone would take the trouble of asking him directly what had happened to him. Instead, the chief exclaimed, "I knew it! There had to be vervets in this whole thing! There is no way this young red tail could be in this mess on his own."

"Excuse me, Chief," Punkey said in a pleading voice. "Since we are all tired, please allow us to go and sleep now. Tomorrow let us gather here, and I will tell you what happened."

The chief begrudgingly agreed. With that, the monkeys went their separate ways, eager for the morning to come so that they could hear the whole story. But even as they left, you could hear most red-tailed parents blaming the vervet kids for messing with their children.

Chapter 14

Punkey and Shulley Speak of Fairness and Equality for All

WHEN MORNING CAME, MANY MONKEYS gathered at the chief's compound to hear Punkey's explanation of what had happened the previous day. The group was even larger than the one that had gathered the previous day.

The chief welcomed all the monkeys and told them that he was happy to see them turn out in such large numbers. He then invited Punkey to come forward. As Punkey made his way to the chief, it was so quiet that the only thing the monkeys could hear was the shuffling of

Punkey's feet, the singing of different kinds of birds in the distance, and the howling of the wind.

Unbeknown to the monkeys, some other animals, who happened to enjoy monkey's meat, had become curious about the gathering. These animals had never seen so many monkeys gathered in one place. A pride of lions hid behind an anthill, waiting for an opportune moment.

A big chimpanzee hid on one edge of the open area that the chief uses to relax, and two leopards hid on the other edge. They were also waiting for the best moment to get their catch for the day. As to top it off, a big snake had gone up the umbrella-like tree and was salivating for a monkey.

Punkey took a deep breath and scanned the multitude of monkeys.

He was amazed at how many monkeys had come to listen to him. He saw his teacher, Miss Pam, as well as the school principal and a good number of his schoolmates. Tears welled up in his eyes when he saw his good friends Sankey and Lankey sitting together. How close he had come to never seeing these two friends again! He looked toward his family and saw Shulley seated between their parents. Beyond them, he saw members of the MPF and the 8S and their leaders. These tough monkeys had biceps so hard you could break a stone on them.

Punkey Asks a Strange Question

Punkey thanked the chief for giving him this rare opportunity to address such a large crowd. Then he took a deep breath and asked, "Vervets, do you genuinely love and always treat each other fairly?"

The monkeys looked at each other, confused. They had thought that the purpose of the gathering was for Punkey to explain the events that had led to his wearing a leopard skin and to point out the vervet who had misled him into using the root powder. Why was he asking such a strange question?

Punkey knelt down, pointed at the chief, took a deep breath, and courageously asked, "Chief, do you genuinely love vervet monkeys and always treat them fairly?"

A flutter of whisperings and hushed noises came from the audience. The chief looked flustered and didn't answer. A calm Punkey then looked at the leaders of the MPF and the 8S, who had sat together, and repeated the question. "Sirs, do you genuinely love vervets and always treat them fairly?"

An impatient red-tailed monkey from the audience shouted, "Little fellow, don't waste our time. We came here to hear how you got that leopard skin!"

Another echoed, "And we want to know who the vervets are that misled you to take the stuff. You know what I mean!"

All eyes were fixed on Punkey. He turned to look at the entire audience and repeated the question. "To all the red-tailed monkeys who are here, do you always treat vervets fairly?"

Many of the monkeys became restless and began to get angry.

After some silence, Punkey said, "If you red tails are honest, you know that you don't always treat vervets fairly." Punkey cleared his throat. "Yesterday, I was very hurt when the conclusion was drawn that it was my vervet friends, Sankey and Lankey, who had influenced me to use the root powder." Punkey paused and then said, "That is far from the truth." He looked uneasily at the crowd. "Those sentiments have been repeated today. Fellow monkeys, these conclusions are a result of what I call *monkeyism*. No vervet was involved in influencing me to use the root powder."

"What are you saying, Punkey?" the chief asked.

"What I am saying, Chief, is that it was not my vervet friends, Sankey and Lankey, or any vervet who taught me to use the root powder. It was a fellow red-tailed monkey that introduced me to the root."

The crowd was silent. Punkey's eyes shifted from the chief to his family to the crowd and back to the chief. He took a deep breath and continued, "Chief, yesterday my family and I returned from a vacation where we visited with some red-tailed family friends. While we were there, my new friend—the son of the family—introduced me to the powdered root. That was when I first seriously used the root, and I enjoyed it. Every day, for two weeks, we chewed the root and sniffed and sometimes smoked its powder. I fell in love with it.

"Before my family started for home, my friend gave me some powder, and I hid it in my fur." He pointed at his belly. "I used some of the root powder on the return journey, and it made me so daring that I did something reckless and stupid, almost costing me my life!"

"But, Punkey," his mother exclaimed, "you promised you would never use the root again! What's going on?"

Punkey looked sadly at his parents. "When we got back yesterday, I met up with my friends Sankey and Lankey, and I told them about the powder. I disregarded my promise never to use it again and tried to convince my friends of the pleasures of the root. After much persuasion, Lankey agreed to use it, but Sankey refused. And that's how I landed in the mess with the Maasai and the leopard skin."

An emotional Punkey looked at the audience and said, "As you now know, it was a red tail who introduced me to the root powder, and it was I—another red tail—who introduced it to my friend. But all of you automatically assumed it was a vervet who did it."

Punkey looked solemn. "That is why I asked the question, 'Do you always treat vervets fairly?' because deep in our hearts we know we don't. A vervet is as good a monkey as any. But years of prejudice and years of the law being applied unfairly have hampered vervets' progress and discouraged many of them."

Shulley Speaks Up

The chief shook his head and made some gruff noises in his throat. Before he could say anything, a red-tailed monkey from the audience shouted defiantly, "I don't believe anything you have said!"

"What is it that I've said that you don't believe?" Punkey asked, sounding a little impatient. "That a red tail taught me how to use the root, or that the laws are applied differently to vervets so as to oppress them?"

The monkey did not answer.

Punkey took a deep breath and continued, "Overcoming a problem begins by accepting that it exists. If we refuse to accept that we have a problem, then we will not overcome it. We need to accept the fact that there is bad blood between red tails and vervets. If we fail to do this, we will never overcome monkeyism."

Shulley stood up. "Chief, may I say something?" She rubbed her hands together as she politely awaited the chief's response. He seemed to be struggling to make up his mind. Eventually he nodded and indicated that she should speak.

Shulley smiled and took a deep breath. "The Maasai Mara would be a greater place than it is now if only we were fair to each other," she said. "There is no way we can enjoy genuine success when there are some groups of monkeys, especially the vervets, cornered into poverty and suffering. We cannot oppress our own, denying them access to basic rights and forcing them into crime and negative behaviors, and then turn around and blame them for their antisocial behavior. If Lankey were to speak, you would be shocked to hear what he has gone through.

"We need to level the playing field. We need fairness, justice, and equality for all!" Shulley's voice shook a little. A loud murmuring rose as the monkeys voiced their opinions to one another.

The chief clapped his hands to get the monkeys' attention. "Shulley," he said, "although I don't totally agree with you—because I don't believe that we red tails have anything to do with the vervets being cornered into whatever corner they are in—what you have said kind of makes sense. It is possible that many vervets *have* been forced to find their way into crime or don't know how to advance forward because of the negative things they consistently hear about them."

Several monkeys in the group nodded. One red tail said, "I believe she is right, Chief. To keep pretending that things are okay in the Maasai Mara will not help us. We need to take the bull by the horns—the bull of monkeyism. Only then will we have genuine success."

"I can testify to what Shulley has said," Miss Pam called out from the audience. "We need to learn to love each other, to understand each other, and to trust each other. We need to learn to live in unity. This is what the Maasai Mara needs. These things will not come naturally. *We need to learn them!*"

"Thank you, Miss Pam, for what you have said," Punkey said. "There are many negative things in life that we cannot fix immediately, but aiming for fairness and justice for all is one thing that we can begin to do immediately."

"Chief," Shulley said, looking straight into the chief's eyes, "the use of root powder and the antisocial behavior manifested in our society as a whole—and not only among vervets, as we too often choose to believe—is a symptom of the failure of community leadership. If we continue to use the same methods over and over"—she paused to see if she had everybody's attention—"the end result in our society will always be the same: a degenerating society. We need to change our approach."

She took a deep breath and said, "May I conclude with these words. Let us all realize that we are a family. The Power that designed us to be together believes that we can live together. Let us make an effort to learn to live for one another. We are brothers and sisters. Our success depends on leaning on each other. Let's join our hands and work together. There is more to us than just our fur. It is fur-deep thinking to believe that the only thing that makes us is our fur, and fur is not very deep. When we get injured, our pain is the same. Our blood is the same. And when we die, our death is the same. Our exit from the Maasai Mara, when we finally breathe our last, will be the same. Let us speak the language of unity. Let us preach the message of togetherness. To all of us young ones, let us show the Maasai Mara that we are a generation on a mission, determined to overcome the behavior that is showing signs of reaching its end as intelligence and commonsense thinking take over. And to all of us, let those who see us and hear us speak see evidence that we are one family of the Maasai Mara."

The chief did not respond, but if it had been possible to see the inner workings of his mind, the watching monkeys would have seen that big changes were taking place in their chief's mind.

Chapter 15

Sankey and Lankey's Heart-to-Heart Talk with the Vervets

SANKEY STOOD UP AND ASKED the chief if he and Lankey could say a few words. The chief, who had become very quiet and thoughtful, nodded in agreement.

"Lankey and I appreciate what Punkey and Shulley have said," Sankey said. "It is very true. As vervets, we have been oppressed for as long as we can remember. Red tails have used every trick under the sun to push us down to the bottom of the barrel. And, surely, we are now at rock bottom."

"If you were to visit our areas, you would notice that we don't have good schools," Lankey said. "There are no beautiful parks in our areas. Many of our things are run down and are never repaired." An emotional Lankey vented his frustrations.

Sankey ran his fingers through the fur on the side of his head as he said, "In addition to this, while you may not agree with me, from the perspective of us vervets, the laws of this land are not applied fairly across the board—that is, the law is applied differently to vervets and red tails."

"In case you have chosen not to understand what Sankey has said, let me explain it this way," Lankey said while pushing his fists together. "I remember one day Miss Pam was teaching us mathematics." He smiled across at Miss Pam, who was seated on the opposite side of the crowd. She nervously smiled back, unsure of what Lankey was going to say.

Lankey continued, "She took us to a sandy place and asked us to stand in two groups facing each other some distance apart. Then she drew something in the sand between us. She asked one group to describe what it was that she had drawn, and that group said it was the top end of a walking stick, like those used by the Maasai people. She then turned to the other group and asked them the same question. Without hesitation, the other group said she had drawn one of those hooks tourists use to catch fish in the Mara River. Isn't it amazing that the same object could be viewed so differently?"

The crowd of monkeys looked blankly at Lankey, wondering where he was going with this illustration. As if he had read their minds, he cleared his throat and said, "Just as this single object was viewed in two totally different ways, laws in the Maasai Mara have unfortunately been applied in different ways. Depending on the officer, the law can be … er …" Lankey stammered a little, as if he did not want to continue with his train of thought. But then he shook his body as if shaking water from his fur, looked at the MPF, and continued, "I mean that the same law can be interpreted as a Maasai's walking stick or as a tourist's hook, depending on who it is being applied to. And due to this unfair approach, many innocent monkeys, including red tails but especially vervets, have suffered a great deal."

An angry member from the MPF yelled, "I don't think you know what you're talking about! You don't know how dangerous our job is. We put our lives on the line for all monkeys on a daily basis!"

Shulley Shares a Story

Shulley quickly interrupted the speaker, coming to Lankey's rescue. "As a red-tailed monkey," she said, "I have witnessed these different ways of implementing the law. Once I was walking along the Mara River together with two of my vervet friends." Shulley hesitated. Just like Lankey, she appeared to want to discontinue speaking but then gathered the courage to proceed. "We were stopped by two red-tailed MPF officers," she said, pointing toward where the MPF officers were sitting. "They searched my two vervet friends in a way that clearly showed they had no respect for them. I tried to ask the MPF officers what was going on. They told me that they knew what they were doing and that I should stay out of it, as it was none of my business.

"Then suddenly one of them exclaimed, 'I knew it!' He waved his hand in the air. 'You were accusing us of being unfair to them,' he said as he walked toward me, 'but what is this?' He waved a rolled leaf into my face. I asked him what it was, and he grinned and told me that it was root powder.

"'No! That can't be true!' my friend said. Shaken and terrified, my friend cried and pleaded and said, 'I don't know what is going on. I have never used root powder in my life!'

"The MPF officers paid no attention. They tied her hands behind her back and began to drag her away. I ran after them, trying to persuade them to let her go, as there must be some mistake. One of the MPF officers turned to me, his face distorted with anger as if he were experiencing pain from thirty toothaches. He grabbed my arm, shook me, and muttered angrily under his breath, 'If you continue disturbing us, we will do to you what we have done to her!'"

Shulley stopped speaking. She was overcome with emotion. Then, wiping tears off her face, she said, "I am unable to continue. I will have to finish it next time."

By this time, Lankey had moved over next to Shulley and had put his arm around her to comfort her. He turned to the audience. "Can you believe it? The MPF actually planted the root powder on this innocent monkey and subjected her to such cruel treatment when they knew in their heart of hearts that she was innocent! The reason they did it? Because she was a vervet. They knew that the other monkeys would believe their story because vervets are infamous for using the root. This is not fair!" Lankey said, wiping away tears from his eyes.

Lankey Shares a Story

"Does the law have a face? Does the law have a color? How can we twist the law like this? When vervets hear these stories, how are they supposed to trust the MPF?" Lankey asked, his voice burdened with emotion. His lips quivering with anger, he asked, "How many of you remember the incident of the young vervet who was given bananas by an old red-tailed monkey?" Lankey scanned the crowd. Some raised their hands, but others just looked at him blankly. "For the sake of those who don't know the story, let me tell you what happened," Lankey said as he sadly shook his head from side to side.

"One day, an old red-tailed monkey picked up a bunch of bananas that had fallen from a Maasai man's bicycle as he rode along. The old monkey saw a young vervet monkey in the distance and called him over. The old monkey asked the vervet to deliver the bananas to the MPF and explain that a Maasai man had dropped them. The old red tail then went on his way. The young vervet ran toward the rocks where the MPF officers worked, but before he got there, two red-tailed MPF officers, who were in a tree scouting the area, saw him and asked him to stop. The young vervet stopped and smiled at the MPF officers. The two monkeys climbed out of the tree and asked him where he was headed.

"Innocence written all over his face, he told them that some old monkey had seen a Maasai man drop the bananas and had asked him to take them to the MPF. The officers did not believe his story. They said to him, 'We know vervets. You are all born evil. You must have stolen the bananas from the Maasai!' The young vervet tried to explain, but they told him that the more he protested, the more trouble he would get himself into. They grabbed the bananas, tied them on his head and tied his hands.

"They beat him as they led him to their workplace, and with his hands tied, he could not defend himself. By the time they arrived at the rocks where they worked, the young monkey was in bad shape, his left leg broken." There were gasps of dismay from the crowd as Lankey paused. He cleared his throat.

"When monkeys heard crying, they came running from every direction. A large group of different kinds of monkeys gathered at the MPF workplace. When the parents of the young monkey saw that it was their son lying in a pool of blood, they wailed and tried to run to him, but the MPF officers shoved them away. The other monkeys asked what had happened for the young monkey to have been beaten like that. The MPF officers said that the monkey had stolen bananas from the Maasai people and had then tried to fool the officers with a story about getting the bananas from somebody who had seen a Maasai man drop them.

"The old monkey—the one who had picked up the bananas in the first place—had also heard the crying, but, being old, he was the last to arrive on the scene. He couldn't believe what he saw. The young monkey had almost passed out. The trembling old monkey told the MPF and all who had gathered there that it was he who had sent the boy and that he had seen the Maasai man drop the bananas. He asked the MPF to explain why they had beaten the young monkey. He thought that the law of the Maasai Mara was that a monkey was innocent until proven guilty, but when it came to vervets, it seemed that they were considered guilty until proven innocent! He complained bitterly that what the MPF had done was wrong.

"The monkeys began to shout and throw rocks all over. The leader of the MPF called the old monkey into the cave while other MPF officers tried to control the crowd. No one knows what happened inside the cave, but when the old red tail eventually came out, he walked straight past the wailing parents and away from the crowd, without looking at anyone or saying anything. The MPF untied the young monkey and allowed his father to pick him up."

Lankey took a deep breath and said, "Up to this day, that monkey is crippled and has never been compensated. He is lucky to be alive."

By the time Lankey finished speaking, a number of monkeys had started to cry. Lankey looked at the monkeys for a long time. Then he asked, "Is it a curse to be born a vervet?"

Sankey Gives a Challenge to the Vervets

An emotional Sankey wiped the tears from his eyes. He walked over to Lankey and hugged him. After he had collected himself, he said, "Friends, all that you have heard today regarding the injustices that vervets have experienced is just the tip of the iceberg. There is a lot more." He took a slow, deep breath and then, to the shock of every monkey gathered there, said, "But, vervets, I will not give us the right to feel sorry for ourselves."

Every vervet's eyes opened wide in disbelief. All eyes were focused on Sankey, who was now calm and collected. Sankey continued, "I know what I'm going to say will be painful, especially against the backdrop of what we have just heard, but I will say it anyway. Yes, we know that vervets have been systematically undermined for as long as the Mara River has been flowing, but, my fellow vervets, to use this as an excuse to do crime and all kinds of other self-inflicted harm to ourselves will not help us. It will get us nowhere. Crime and other problematic behaviors are the wrong way to react to our problems of oppression. The crimes we commit are an indication that we have given up. It shows that we have accepted forever living at the bottom of the barrel and are refusing to try to better ourselves. My fellow vervets, giving up is a misplaced solution. In fact, it is no solution at all!"

Lankey nodded in agreement and chimed in, "And to take out our anger on each other, causing the untimely deaths of fellow vervets, is wrong. Look at all the gangs in the areas in which we live, killing each other every day.

"In the process many innocent monkeys, young and old, are killed. What is our gain? If we are angry with red tails, then why are we killing each other?" Lankey sighed. "I have not done any precise counting, but, friends, it is possible that we may be killing a lot more of each other than the MPF is. I don't know." He shrugged his shoulders. "If we went to our graveyards and did some counting, how many graves would we find of vervets who died at the hands of the MPF, and how many graves would we find of vervets who died at the hands of fellow vervets?" He scanned the audience. "I don't have the answer, but at the end of the day, whether our deaths are caused by the MPF or by other vervets, death is death," Lankey said, his voice pleading. "Our families hurt no matter who inflicts the death!"

A solemn Sankey pleaded, "Fellow vervets, the time has come for us to set our future right. Let us not allow our past to control our future. We have no control over the past, but we have control over the future. No one can successfully run forward if they keep looking behind. Our past is only important in helping us to understand how best to map our way forward. We can look back for reference, but we cannot camp in the past. Our eyes should constantly be focused ahead."

Sankey noticed Lankey looking eager to speak and asked, "What's on your mind, Lankey?"

A faint smile danced on Lankey's lips as he said, "I have seen tourists play with something round like a fruit. I don't know what it is, but when they throw it to the ground, it bounces straight up, and they catch it." He pretended to throw something to the ground and catch it. "I've noticed that the harder they throw it to the ground, the faster and higher it bounces up, many times bouncing much higher than them."

"I like what I'm hearing," Sankey said. "Fellow vervets, I hope you get the meaning of what Lankey has said. The harder we have been thrown down, the higher we are supposed to rise."

"That's exactly it!" Lankey exclaimed. "Remember that for every action there is an equal and opposite reaction. We are not supposed to remain down. We *must* bounce back!" His eyes sparkled with excitement as he contemplated this exhilarating idea.

Sankey Honors His Mother

Sankey scanned the crowd until he spotted his mother. He smiled and said, "Mom, please come forward." His mother walked forward, not too sure what her son wanted her to say. When she got to his side, he hugged her, looked at the monkeys, and said, "I would like to thank my mother in your hearing. My father and my sister died a long time ago. Many of my classmates know how they died; those of you who want to know more can ask me privately." He looked sad. "I have grown up with a single parent, but she has done a sterling job of raising me. One of the things my mom has consistently done is warn me not to use the powder that led to my dad's death. Many times I have been tempted to use the root powder when I've seen my friends enjoying it and having fun. But my mom's words always ring in my mind. I am proud to say I have followed her counsel." Sankey's mother wiped a tear from the corner of her eye.

Sankey continued, "What has made it easier to listen to my mother is that she teaches me by example. She doesn't do any of the things she expects me not to do." He looked out over the audience. "Parents, by not using the root and getting involved in bad habits, it gives you the moral authority to tell your children not to do those things. I have learned from my mother that teaching by example is the only effective way to teach.

"Another thing that my mother has done for me is to never hesitate to correct me when I'm wrong. At first I resented her correction and thought that she was an unloving mom." He turned to his mother. "Mom, many times I mistakenly thought you didn't love me when you didn't defend me after I had done something wrong." He looked at the audience and teased, "She always sided with the teachers." He squeezed his mother tight. "But I soon realized that it was because she loved me that she would not make excuses for me." Sankey's mother beamed with pride.

"I remember the day I told my mother that some red-tailed monkeys had treated me unfairly. I was fed up and wanted to leave school," Sankey said, looking first at the audience and then at his mom. "She told me that the way to deal with red-tailed monkeys is to remain in school and to work hard. She told me that by doing this I would be proving to the red tails that we have the same kind of brain—that I am in no way inferior to them. Since then I have tried to share this lesson with my fellow vervets."

Sankey continued, "When it comes to the law of the land, my mother has told me over and over that it does not pay to be on the wrong side of the law or to pick fights with the MPF." He turned to his mother and said, "Thank you for your firm counsel. Some of my friends are locked up for breaking the law, and some of my friends are dead, most of them killed not by any red tail or the MPF but by other vervets in gang-related violence. I am so grateful that because of you I have escaped such fates." He gave her a big squeeze.

Instead of returning to her seat, Sankey's mother turned to her son and asked, "May I say something?"

Sankey held out his arm in a gesture of welcome and said, "Please do. The more the better!" He stepped back as his mother took center stage.

"Chief and all of you who are here," she said, "I have taught my son, Sankey, that not all the red tails hate us and not all the MPF officers are bad. There are many red tails who sympathize with us and understand our experience." She paused as many vervets and red tails applauded. "I have taught Sankey that no matter what the red tails try to do, they will not have the energy to hold us down forever. I have encouraged him to look around and see how more and more vervets are occupying leadership positions here in the Maasai Mara."

Sankey's mother waved her hand high in the air as she said at the top of her voice, "Young vervets, don't give up! Let us not give the red tails an excuse to continue oppressing us. Keep pressing on, though you are hurting and lonely. Keep pressing on, though there seems to be no hope in sight. Keep pressing on, though tears dim your eyesight. It is only determination that will take us forward. As somebody said earlier on, change will not happen overnight. Therefore, young vervets, keep pressing on. Let us give the red tails a run for their money!"

Sankey clapped and cheered as his mother returned to her seat amid thunderous applause.

Chapter 16

Punkey Defines Power

PUNKEY, A CHEERFUL SMILE BRIGHTENING his face, asked the gathered crowd, "By the way, have I told you yet how I ended up with a leopard skin?"

The audience looked at each other in surprise and then replied with a resounding "No!"

"Tell us how it happened," the chief said. "All we know is that when Lankey and Sankey last saw you, a Maasai man was holding a knife to your neck. We all concluded that you had been killed!"

"Well, I also expected to be dead by now," Punkey said, "but what I witnessed instead was a mind-awakening definition of power."

"What do you mean?" the chief asked, looking baffled.

Punkey told the audience of how, as soon as he and his family had returned from vacation, he'd gone looking for his friends Sankey and Lankey. He told of how he'd tried to persuade both of them to use the root but only Lankey had accepted.

Punkey stopped and looked at the chief and the audience. The whole crowd said almost together, "Go on!"

Punkey continued, "As the powder did its damage in our bodies, we heard music coming from the Maasai village, and in our stupor, we decided to go and check things out. To our delight, we saw behind an inkajijik three big pots from which the Maasai people were taking nuts. When the people left, Lankey and I went down to go and steal some peanuts, although Sankey did try to warn us against this foolishness." Punkey gave Sankey a knowing look.

"Because we were under the influence of the root, we were not reasoning well. Our hands got stuck in the big pots with the narrow necks. Oh, we were scared! When the Maasai man returned, he grabbed both of us, but Lankey managed to escape after scratching the Maasai man's face and climbed up a tree. But I could not escape, because the man had tied my hands and feet tightly." Many in the audience were holding their breath as they listened to Punkey's thrilling story.

"When the man's wife and his children appeared, they were delighted to see me tied up and helpless in the man's hands. The man then placed a large knife to my throat. When Sankey and Lankey saw the knife, they took off." Punkey looked at his two friends and smiled. "At the time I thought they were abandoning me, but I'm glad to hear that it was because they wanted to get help.

"For some reason the Maasai man decided not to kill me. He took me to some old man's inkajijik. The old man took me and the knife, and again I had the knife placed against my throat! But for some unknown reason, he also changed his mind. He went inside his inkajijik and came out with that leopard skin. Then he sewed it on me and let me loose." Punkey shook his head in relief.

"It was only later on, after the root cleared from my head, that I came to realize that the three pots were a trap. Probably things were being stolen from the inkajijik, and they wanted to catch the culprits. Because they had caught me in the act, they concluded it was me who had been stealing their things, even though that wasn't the case."

Punkey paused momentarily to catch his breath as the monkeys anxiously waited to hear what he would say next. "They had every right to chop my head off," Punkey said, fear written all over his face, "but they gave me the benefit of the doubt." He paused again before he said, "This is what I define as power."

The monkeys looked at each other in confusion. "What kind of power is that?" an angry MPF officer demanded.

Punkey looked at the MPF and replied, "What I learned from this experience is that a powerful monkey is the one who has the power to do whatever he wants, including the power to kill another monkey who has committed a crime, but has trained himself to hold back his power and look for other ways of dealing with situations."

Punkey took a deep breath and said, "If you don't have the power to control your power, then you are not powerful. I have come to believe that all the leaders in the Maasai Mara—at whatever level, parents included—need to live this definition of power. It is only controlled power that will maximize positive outcomes in the Maasai Mara."

Silence rested upon the audience. The monkeys looked at each other amid scattered applause.

"Punkey, that is an interesting definition of power," the chief said. "I think I'm beginning to see sense in it."

"Just imagine if the Maasai people had killed me instead of giving me another chance," Punkey said. "I'm not a habitual thief, and neither am I a frequent user of the powder. It was only childishness and foolishness that made me do the things I did. I am thankful they chose to punish me differently. They chose a form of punishment that would bring positive discipline and give me a second chance. If they had killed me, it would not have solved even the tip of the iceberg of the powder-use problem, especially when you consider that the boy who introduced me to the powder would still be alive on the other side of the Mara River."

Punkey hesitantly opened his mouth and said, "I'm not saying that all monkeys are first-time offenders and that they're all innocent. That's not my point. What I'm trying to say is, what would be the point of discussing the matter if I were dead?"

Two monkeys stood up and said, "Punkey is speaking a lot of sense. We need to thank those Maasai people for using their power in the way Punkey has described to us."

Sounds of agreement came from many in the audience, but not all the monkeys were convinced.

An Angry Vervet Makes an Unexpected Statement

Suddenly an angry vervet bellowed out, "But what about the way the MPF holds power over us? You've heard how Sankey's innocent sister was killed by red-tailed MPF officers." The angry monkey wagged a condemning finger at the red-tailed MPF officers in the audience. His chest heaved up and down.

"You've heard how these MPF officers almost killed an innocent young monkey for simply carrying some bananas. And you've also heard how they planted root powder on Shulley's friend." His hands began to shake as if he had caught a fever.

Scanning the audience, he took a slow, deep breath and said, "This is not right. We are tired of these injustices. To make things worse, the chief and his team seem not to care. They've done nothing about it. We are sick and tired of dealing with issues of bias and hatred and of being sidelined. In short, we are tired of monkeyism."

The vervet monkey stammered, "Our young ones live in fear. Many kids, when they see an MPF officer coming, they run away. They no longer trust the system. At the rate they are being slaughtered, I fear for our future. And even the adults, we also live in fear. We no longer have freedom in our own Maasai Mara. We cannot live like this!" There was a tremor in his voice.

Wrinkles of anger creased the vervet's forehead as he continued, "It is disturbing that the very monkeys who are supposed to protect us are the ones who are killing us!" He took a deep breath, speaking slowly and emphatically while repeatedly pulling fur from his chest.

"Fellow vervets, I think it is time we took justice into our own hands. We need to kill these red-tailed MPF officers and totally wipe them out before they wipe us out!" He glared intimidatingly at the group of MPF officers in the audience.

As the monkeys digested what they had just heard, total silence rested upon the crowd. Though everyone knew about the discrimination and unfairness with which the MPF treated vervets, this was the first time someone had publicly voiced the call to fight back.

A surprised Sankey took a deep breath and looked at the vervet who had just spoken. He then looked at Punkey, Shulley, and Lankey and asked, "What do you say, guys? Do you think killing the MPF officers is a solution to these injustices?"

Shulley looked straight into Sankey's eyes and said, "Well, I don't know whether I should say this or not, but ..." She hesitated a little before continuing, "You're the one who lost a sister, so I think we should hear your views on the matter."

Sankey looked at his mother in the audience, then at the audience itself, then at the vervet who had raised the issue, then at the chief, and finally back at his three friends. Looking squarely at Shulley, he said, "Shulley, you have placed me between a rock and a hard place." He glanced over at the group of MPF officers.

"I have heard from a number of vervets, as well as from some of my red-tail friends, that MPF officers don't feel safe with us vervets," Sankey said. Some monkeys in the audience nodded in agreement.

One angry red tail shouted, "Definitely they don't feel safe with you guys."

Sankey rubbed his hands together and said, "But what the MPF officers should know is that, at this point in time, we don't feel safe with them either." He sounded angry. "Some of these MPF officers seem to think that one's color has the power to make one evil. Hence they conclude that vervets are evil because of their color. With this kind of thinking, when they see vervets, they conclude that they are naturally evil and extremely dangerous and must be prevented from polluting the Maasai Mara.

"Unfortunately, due to this deep-rooted belief, some innocent vervets have been killed because they were suspected of being up to mischief. Usually, by the time all the facts come to light, the innocent monkey has already been killed, and his or her life cannot be restored."

Sankey's voice broke with emotion as he said, "I strongly believe that my sister died just because she was a vervet. The red-tailed MPF officers can have their own defense as to why they did what they did—I leave that to their conscience. But I believe that all who witnessed what happened, including the MPF officers themselves, know in their heart of hearts that my sister's death was the death of an innocent." Tears welled in Sankey's eyes. "And unfortunately no one can restore her life."

Lankey, Shulley, and Punkey came and stood next to their friend, and Punkey put his hand on Sankey's shoulder. Sankey's mom began to sob too, but she remained seated. Sankey, his voice trembling, asked, "With this kind of thinking demonstrated by some red tails and some red-tail MPF officers, can we be blamed for being tempted to fight back?"

For a while, no one said a word. Then Sankey turned his tearstained face to the audience and said softly, "I know as vervets we are angry because of the brutality we are experiencing. We have the right to be angry. No one can deny the fact that there is a casualness to the killing of vervets that is frightening to many. But remember one thing. There are hundreds of MPF officers who are innocent and who don't mistreat vervets. They protect and will continue to protect us from many dangerous situations. Remember that out there our enemies—the pythons, leopards, lions, and chimpanzees—still exist. If our enemies still exist, we still need the MPF officers—the *good* MPF officers."

Sankey scanned the many faces looking at him. "Do you think it is right for innocent MPF officers to die because of a few who have acted on misguided beliefs?"

Two Wrongs Don't Make a Right

Lankey tapped Sankey on the shoulder, indicating that he wanted to speak. "To the monkey who has led us into this discussion," he said, looking at the angry vervet, "I want you to know that killing the MPF officers, as Sankey has mentioned already, is no solution. Two wrongs do not make a right." He looked at his fellow vervet, remembering when Sankey had spoken this profound truth in Miss Pam's class.

"After all," Lankey continued, "it is simply not possible to kill all the MPF officers, just as it is impossible, no matter how hard they might try, for the hateful MPF officers to kill all of us. We need to realize that this kind of thinking will only continue to fuel distrust. It will take us nowhere."

"I agree," Punkey said, stepping forward. "You cannot stop killing by killing." He paused a moment and then said, "When a Maasai mother wants to put out the fire after she's done her cooking, does she bring more fire to put it out? No! Either she puts water on it, covers it with dirt, or lets it burn itself out while carefully watching it to make sure it doesn't get out of control."

Punkey sighed as he said, "If we were to fight fire with fire, we would only make matters worse. Some monkeys may be dead, but the cause of the problem will still be lingering around, continuing to haunt our Maasai Mara like an evil spirit."

Shulley Talks of Fighting Monkeyism

Shulley stepped forward. "Chief, I believe that the evil spirit Punkey is talking about, the one that is haunting the Maasai Mara, is the monster of monkeyism. If we are going to fight anything, it should be *this* monster."

Shulley continued, "Some of us, whether red tail or vervet, are totally steeped in the mindset of monkeyism. We breathe hate through and through. No MPF or 8S team can rescue us from this beast that has its deadly claws embedded deep in our flesh. Only a reprogramming of our hearts and minds—a new way of seeing things—can release us from its grip."

Shulley's voice rose clear and pure into the warm evening air. "We need to realize that we vervets and red tails have so much in common. Our biggest common denominator is that we are all monkeys. This is what should unite us—not whether we are vervets or red tails!"

Punkey Makes a Startling Suggestion

Punkey had been thoughtfully listening to his sister's words. He now turned to the chief. "Chief," he said politely, "I don't think that the Maasai people care about the differences between vervets and red tails. I'm sure they see our different colors, but at the end of the day the only thing they see is that we are all monkeys."

Punkey, his eyes dancing with excitement at the novelty of what he was about to say, continued, "I think that the only monkeys who should be allowed to have power—whether MPF officers or principals or teachers or any other leadership role—are monkeys who see monkeys as monkeys and nothing else." He looked triumphantly at the audience.

"And how do we do that?" the chief asked.

"Um ... uh ..." Punkey scratched his head, trying desperately to think of a solution.

"I think I can answer that," Shulley said, mercifully coming to her brother's rescue.

"What answer do you have for us?" asked the chief.

"Just as we have exams in our schools, anyone who would like to join the MPF or be chosen for any other leadership role should take an exam," Shulley said.

"What are you talking about?" an angry MPF officer blasted.

Shulley calmly smiled at the angry MPF officer. "The main purpose of the exam would be to reveal the amount of monkeyism a monkey harbors," she said. "Since no one is totally free from monkeyism, a safe level of monkeyism would need to be determined, and anyone whose levels of monkeyism are above the safe level should not be allowed to be an MPF officer or any other type of leader." Shulley wagged her finger to emphasize her point.

"Chief, I would like to add to what Shulley has just suggested," Sankey said. "Perhaps it would also be a good idea to develop a code of power (the kind that Punkey described), love, and conduct to be recited by every monkey, every day, at the start of the day. Maybe this will help us to remember that we are all monkeys—nothing more and nothing less. This should go a long way in reducing the amount of hatred and distrust among us."

The chief nodded in approval. "That makes a lot of sense," he said, smiling at the clever friends. "We will definitely look into that." With that, the chief suddenly broke into a song, and joy registered all over his face.

The surprised audience listened as the chief sang of a new Maasai Mara that he saw in his mind's eye where all monkeys would live together in unity. When he finished singing, the audience clapped, and the chief smiled and took a bow.

Chapter 17

The Monkeys Catch the Vision

WITH THE AUDIENCE QUIETLY LOOKING on, Shulley, Punkey, Lankey, and Sankey formed a semicircle and talked to each other in low tones.

Then Sankey walked over to the chief and whispered something into his ear. The chief nodded in approval, waved his right hand in the air, and said loudly, "No problem—go ahead!" Smiling from ear to ear, Sankey thanked the chief and walked back to his friends.

All eyes were on Sankey as he waved his hands in the air and called for all monkeys below the age of six years to come and sit in front of him. The kids, some hesitating a little, jumped up and bulleted to the place where Sankey had pointed. Soon the place was packed with kids.

An enthusiastic and excited Punkey walked over to where the children had gathered and said, "It's great to see such a large group of beautiful kids! Let me tell you about when I was little like you." The children grew quiet as they awaited his story.

"Now, I don't want to embarrass my parents by telling this story," Punkey said, "but I think it will be of great benefit to you. When I was growing up, Lankey, Shulley, and I used to play together at that playground near the school." Punkey pointed in the direction of the playground. His friends nodded as he continued, "But every time we went there, our parents didn't want us to play together."

"I remember it very well," Shulley said, taking up the story. "When we whined, cried, and complained, our parents told us that vervets could not be trusted. They said that vervets were born crooks and therefore a bad influence. That's why they didn't want us to play with Lankey." Some of the children looked as if they knew what she was talking about.

Lankey nodded in agreement and said, "I want all of you young monkeys to listen very carefully. What Punkey and Shulley are saying did not only happen to them." He walked closer to the children. "Whenever Punkey and Shulley's parents called them away, my parents also called me and told me how bad the *red tails* were. I was taught to distrust red tails, and Punkey and Shulley were taught to distrust vervets."

Sankey looked at the chief and the audience and said, "Are you listening, our parents and leaders? These kids are not born hating each other. Hatred is planted in their minds by their parents!"

A red-tailed monkey, lines of anger creasing her face, stood up and said crossly, "What are you trying to say, you little fellas? Your parents were only protecting you from each other! You should know that there are natural unwritten laws within all of us that must be followed." She glared at the young monkeys.

"With all due respect," Punkey said, "could you please tell us exactly which natural unwritten laws you are talking about, ma'am?" Punkey looked her squarely in the face. Some red tails booed him.

The red tail opened her mouth to speak, but before she could answer, Shulley politely interrupted her and said, "As red tails, do we even have the right to respond to this issue?

Do we have the moral authority to even speak out?" Shulley's question challenged the red tail, and she remained quiet.

"Besides," Lankey said, sounding a little annoyed, "laws—whether written or unwritten—are not the issue we are dealing with here. It is not laws and more laws that are going to bring us together. So far, laws have not worked. Laws by themselves will do nothing." Lankey took in a deep breath and continued, "The problem is not with the laws. The problem is with our hearts. Up until now, laws have failed to change our hearts."

"Thank you, Lankey," Punkey said. "You are one hundred percent correct." Turning to the young monkeys, he smiled at them and said, "My fellow young monkeys who are here today, listen to me carefully. I know you love your parents, but let me remind you that your parents will not live forever. One of these days, they will be dead and gone." Punkey paused, shifting his eyes from the children to the adults and youth and then back to the children. "What kind of Maasai Mara do you want to have when you are grown up and your parents are gone?"

He turned to Lankey and Sankey and said, "I want a Maasai Mara where I live in peace with these friends of mine, even though they are not my color. I want a Maasai Mara where I live with all of you in peace, a Maasai Mara where I am valued and respected for being a monkey and not for what monkey group I come from."

"Young monkeys," Shulley said, "we don't want a Maasai Mara where we continue to see other monkeys as lesser than us because they look different from us." She paused before driving her point home. "Color is neutral. It has no feelings of love or hatred. What is to blame is what our parents have planted in our minds regarding our different colors. This is what is destroying the Maasai Mara."

"We are the ones who hold the keys to the future of the Maasai Mara. This place belongs to all of us," Punkey said, looking keenly at the children and the whole audience to see if he was getting through to them.

Lankey spoke up. "Parents, what kind of legacy are you going to leave behind? How will the Maasai Mara remember you? What will others and your children say of you when you are long gone? Will you be happy to have done what you have done?"

Some of the adults were shaking their heads, and some were looking down in shame.

"But even if the adults have failed us," Shulley encouraged, "as children, we can bring about change for the better!"

A Young Monkey Shares Miss Pam's Lessons about Mosquitoes

Sankey looked down at the eager young faces and said, "Maybe you are saying to yourself, 'I am very small—too small to bring any meaningful change!' But let me tell you, size does not matter!" He paused a moment. "Those of you who have been in Miss Pam's class will remember her lessons about mosquitoes."

Some of the kids smiled and nodded.

"Does anyone remember what Miss Pam said about mosquitoes?" Sankey asked, smiling back at the kids. A very small girl, a vervet, shot her hand up. Sankey looked at her and said, "Yes?"

With radiant eyes and a smile that could have lit up the whole Maasai Mara, the girl sprang up and said, "I remember all six points Miss Pam told us," she said, her eyes sparkling with confidence.

All the monkeys stretched their necks to see the girl. "Go ahead," Sankey said, giving her the green light.

"Here are the six points," the young monkey said, confidence radiating from her whole being. "Point number one: although mosquitos are extremely tiny, when they enter the cave where you're sleeping, they will make your sleep miserable."

In the audience, Miss Pam was all smiles.

"Miss Pam said that a mosquito will give any giant a sleepless night, untold misery, and much discomfort," the girl continued. "A mosquito will make you hit yourself continuously and make you jump up from your comfortable place of sleep and go chasing it around trying to kill it," the girl said as she imitated chasing a mosquito.

The audience laughed, enjoying her energy and enthusiasm. She continued, "It does not take long for you to realize that this little creature the mosquito can make a big difference to your sleep." She looked around, smiling sweetly as the audience quieted down. She licked her lips and slowly said, "A mosquito, although small, does not despise itself. It thinks big. Size means nothing to it. This little creature is never intimidated."

"Does anyone remember another point?" Sankey asked, looking around.

"Hey, wait!" the girl said. "I said I remember all six points, and I've only mentioned one!" The girl looked crossly at Sankey, wondering why he would let somebody else steal her show. He shrugged, and all the monkeys chuckled as the girl continued to speak confidently.

"Miss Pam also said that although mosquitos breed in different bodies of water, it does not affect their unity of purpose and mission." The girl wore a big smile as the adults looked at her in amazement. "Some breed in the Mara River. Others breed in ponds or in tins or in the Maasai people's clay pots. And yet others breed in swampy areas. Anywhere water is collected becomes a mosquito's breeding place," the girl said. "And mosquitoes don't have exactly the same color either. But coming from different breeding places and not having the same color does not destroy the unity of these tiny creatures. When they meet in a cave, they don't waste their time debating their origin. They see each other as mosquitoes, and their focus is to annoy you."

Sankey laughed. "That's very true," he said, waving his hand in approval at the girl. Most of the monkeys cheered in agreement, encouraging the girl to continue. Others whispered to each other, saying that what Miss Pam taught her students was very true.

"The third point Miss Pam told us is that mosquitoes cause malaria, a disease that the tourists suffer from. Miss Pam said that many people die because of malaria." The young girl stopped, seeming to forget the rest of the points. She stuck her finger in her mouth, thinking.

"Oh, yes!" She was confident again. "Miss Pam also said that mosquitoes are very determined. They never give up. No matter what you do to protect yourself, they will always find a way to get you. It doesn't matter where you're hiding."

"That's very true," Shulley said. "Mosquitoes are determined."

"Now let me give you the last two points," the girl said, blinking fast as if chasing away mosquitoes. "Miss Pam also said that mosquitoes are risk takers. Every trip a mosquito makes is a risk. They have no assurance that they will come back alive, because when they bite you, you try to kill them. And finally, Miss Pam said that mosquitoes are very creative. They always find a way of biting you no matter what you do!" the girl concluded triumphantly.

As soon as she finished speaking, the audience erupted in clapping and cheering. The cute little monkey dazzled the audience one last time with her big white smile, took a bow toward the chief, and sat down.

Shulley Takes Charge

Taking advantage of the situation, Shulley, filled with enthusiasm, said, "Chief and all of you who are here, we want you to know that though we are small"—she pointed at her fellow young monkeys—"just like mosquitoes, we can make a difference." Turning to the kids, she instructed, "When I say something, I want you to respond by saying, 'Like mosquitoes, we can make a change!' Can you do that? Are you ready?"

All the young monkeys eagerly nodded and responded with a loud "Yes!"

"Though we are just little monkeys ..." Shulley said.

"Like mosquitoes, we can make a change!" all the young monkeys responded.

"Though our problems are much bigger than us ..."

"Like mosquitoes, we can make a change!"

"Though there has been hatred between vervets and red tails ..."

"Like mosquitoes, we can make a change!"

"Knowing that we are the raw materials, the building blocks of the Maasai Mara ..."

"Like mosquitoes, we can make a change!"

"Knowing that we are capable of bringing love and unity to the Maasai Mara ..."

"Like mosquitoes, we can make a change!"

"Knowing that no one is going to build the Maasai Mara for us ..."

"Like mosquitoes, we can make a change!"

"Though we are just little monkeys, we know we can be game changers and agents of change ..."

"Like mosquitoes, we can make a change!"

"Although throughout our childhoods we have been influenced not to love and trust each other ..."

"Like mosquitoes, we can make a change!"

Unexpectedly, just like a big choir, the young monkeys began to chant, "Change is in the air! We can make a change!"

They chanted over and over until the chief rose and began walking over to Sankey, Shulley, Punkey, and Sankey. He turned to face the vast group of monkeys. Everyone was silent, waiting to hear what their chief would say.

"This meeting has changed the Maasai Mara," the chief said, emotion in his voice. "I am convinced that the Maasai Mara will not be the same. Change is in the air. As our voices rise to a crescendo of oneness, burying monkeyism and putting aside our insecurities, fears, and suspicions that destroy our fiber of unity, change is no longer going to be a choice. It is going to be our way of life. These young children standing before you—this is where our strength lies. Parents, let us join our children. Let us believe in our children. We can do it! Let us support our children in making a change."

Following the lead of their chief, the adults began to chant, "Change is in the air! We can make a change!" The young monkeys joined the adults, once again erupting into chanting. A great rhythmic noise rose into the air, filling the Maasai Mara sky, as the entire group shouted, "Change is in the air! We can make a change!"

Unity Is Put to the Test

When the pride of lions hiding behind the anthill, the leopards and the chimpanzee hiding in the bushes, and the snake up in the tree heard the chanting, they slowly began to move toward the monkeys. The predators believed that now was their chance, with the monkeys being so distracted with all this talk of change. Without warning, they pounced on the monkeys from all directions.

The happy chanting turned into the noise of confusion. A large male lion leaped on one of the red-tailed MPF officers and began to drag him away. The other lions targeted other MPF officers, and each of the leopards grabbed a vervet monkey by the neck. The snake coiled itself around the young vervet girl who had given the six lessons about mosquitoes, trapping her in its grip. And the chimpanzee leaped on the chief, crushing him with its massive body.

Instantly, all the monkeys, big and small, vervets and red tails, went on the attack.

One group jumped on the lions, scratching and biting, doing all kinds of somersaults and acrobatic leaps on the lions' backs. The big cats were totally confused and terrified. Another group of monkeys went for the leopards, barking wildly while slapping and throwing stones at them. Another group went for the snake, biting it and beating it with sticks. Other monkeys, armed with sticks, stones, and their sharp teeth, began to beat the chimpanzee. The intruders, realizing that they were outnumbered, fled for their lives, the monkeys in hot pursuit.

As each group returned from chasing the predators, their triumphant voices filled the air of the Maasai Mara as they chanted, "We have done it! We have done it!" They were exhilarated to realize that they were no longer divided into red tails and vervets. They were just one large, united group of monkeys.

When they all gathered together, the shaken chief, thankful to be alive, raised his hand, and silence rested upon the audience. Smiling from ear to ear, the chief said, "We have managed to overcome our enemies because we were united. We did not care who was being attacked—what mattered was saving monkeys. Going forward, this will be the spirit of the Maasai Mara."

Lankey waved his fists up in the air and shouted, "Hooray! From now on we will live for one another. Hand in hand we will walk together. Monkeyism is defeated. Vervets and red tails are now united. The Maasai Mara is no longer divided based on color or differing ideas. Hooray!"

As all the monkeys cheered, Shulley scampered over to Sankey, Lankey, and Punkey and said something to them. Their eyes lit up, and they vigorously nodded in approval. Shulley opened her mouth, her powerful and beautiful voice wafting into the air as she began to sing "Happy, Happy, inside Me."

I'm very happy, happy, happy, happy, inside me.
Happy, happy, happy, happy, inside me.
I'm very happy, happy, happy, happy, inside me.
Happy, happy, inside me,
for monkeyism is defeated.
The Maasai Mara won't be the same.
Yes, vervets, red tails, now united.
Happy, happy, inside me.
From now we'll live for one another.
Hand in hand, we'll walk together,
monkeyism gone forever.
Happy, happy, inside me.

Sankey, Lankey, and Punkey joined in with her song.

Happy, happy, happy, happy, inside me.
Monkeyism is gone forever.

Happy, happy, happy, happy, inside me.
We are determined to work together.
Happy, happy, happy, inside me.
Monkeyism is now hist'ry.
Happy, happy, happy, inside me.
Happy, happy, inside me.

The rest of the monkeys joined in.

I'm very happy, happy, happy, happy, inside me.
Happy, happy, happy, happy, inside me.
I'm very happy, happy, happy, happy, inside me.
Happy, happy, inside me,
for monkeyism is defeated.
The Maasai Mara won't be the same.
Yes, vervets, red tails, now united.
Happy, happy, inside me.
From now we'll live for one another.
Hand in hand, we walk together,
monkeyism gone forever.
Happy, happy, inside me.
Happy, happy, inside me.
Happy, happy, inside me.

Score

Happy Inside Me

Saustin Mfune

Happy Inside Me

Saustin S. K. Mfune

Happy Inside Me

one a-no-ther. Yes, hand in hand, we'll walk to-get-her. Hap-py, hap-py in-side me.

Hap-py, Hap-py, Hap-py, Hap-py in-side me. Mon-key - ism

4

Happy Inside Me

Saustin S. K. Mfune

Happy Inside Me

Happy Inside Me

6

136

Saustin S. K. Mfune

Happy Inside Me

7

Printed in the United States
By Bookmasters